Georgia Dept. of Agriculture, Thomas P. Janes

A Manual of Georgia

for the use of immigrants and capitalists

Georgia Dept. of Agriculture, Thomas P. Janes

A Manual of Georgia
for the use of immigrants and capitalists

ISBN/EAN: 9783337239053

Printed in Europe, USA, Canada, Australia, Japan

Cover: Foto ©Andreas Hilbeck / pixelio.de

More available books at **www.hansebooks.com**

FOR THE USE OF

IMMIGRANTS AND CAPITALISTS.

PREPARED UNDER THE DIRECTION OF

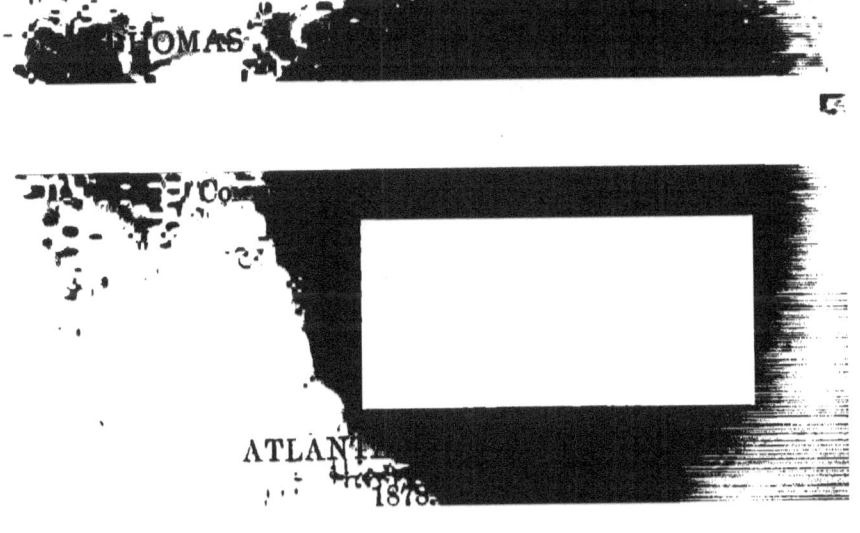

THOMAS

Co

ATLAN

1878.

ERRATA.

On page 7, the 2nd paragraph, commencing with the words, "In nothing regarding us," etc., is the beginning of a chapter on CLIMATE. This title was omitted by the printer, and not observed by the proof-reader, till it was too late to correct it.

On page 36, at the end of the 4th paragraph, the number of students in the Atlanta University is left *blank*. This should have been filled with 244—the number attending the late session.

On the same page, at the end of the 4th line, under the title "Female Colleges," the words "in Georgia" should be *in the world*.

To the list of newspapers in Georgia, (see page 52, 53 and 54) should be added—

Cartersville—*Free Press*, weekly.

Hinesville, (Liberty county)—*Gazette*, weekly.

Dupont, (Clinch county)—*Okeefinokian*, weekly.

There are some typographical errors, but being of minor importance, they are not specially noticed.

MANUAL OF GEORGIA.

INTRODUCTION.

Georgia, although a State of the American Union since the year 1776, when she united with her sister colonies in their memorable struggle for independence of the British Crown, is, perhaps, less known in foreign lands, and to their inhabitants who have sought homes in the Western World, than any other State which engaged with her in the revolution. The cause is readily explained : She lies geographically remote from the old thoroughfares of international commerce ; no lines of steamships have connected her directly with the ports of Europe and, as a consequence, but few immigrants from the Old World have landed on her shores. She has had no public lands to be distributed among railroad corporations and speculators, whose interest was to be advanced by their speedy settlement with a new and industrious population. She has had no Immigration Aid Societies, so abundant in the Northern States of the Union, and no Immigration Agents, who swarm over Europe from the same section, to publish her unrivaled advantages to the world. Peaceful and prosperous until the late civil war consumed her wealth and drenched the land with the blood of her people ; with labor abundant, its natural increase unexampled, and its rewards satisfactory, Georgia had no motive to seek immigration from foreign lands. Her prosperity needed no building up. She asked for no foreign capital for she had an abundance of her own.

Still another reason is to be found in the peculiar labor system of the Southern States, including Georgia, in former years. During the existence of African slavery the people cultivated large farms or plantations—in many instances thousands of acres under one proprietorship—and as the number of slaves increased annually, with prosperous farmers, they preferred rather to add to, than to part with any portion of their landed possessesions. Under the free labor system, requiring a closer personal supervison from proprietors, the latter have found it to their interest to cultivate small farms in preference to large ones ; hence, land is in less demand, larger quantities are on the market at greatly reduced prices, and an increase of population has become desirable.

Such are some of the reasons why Georgia has been content heretofore to pursue the even tenor of her way, and to work out her own destiny within herself. Unaided, she had come to acquire the proud title of " Empire State of the South," which, of itself, is an eloquent testimonial to her material wealth, her political and moral standing, her intelligence and her energy, as compared with her sister States of the southern division of the Union.

But the results of late, long and disastrous war, have sadly changed this happy aspect of affairs. Her territory was desolated, her better class of population reduced in numbers, her accumulated wealth swept away, her social institutions revolutionized, and for a time reversed, and her labor system broken up. Her natural resources, her energy and her love of liberty, alone, remained unimpaired. Her government has been restored to a healthful condition, and law and justice obtain throughout her borders. But her labor system is not well organized, and her capital seriously reduced in amount; as a necessary consequence, a large portion of her fertile fields is uncultivated, her exhaustless mines of the useful and precious metals are but partially worked, and her noble forests of timber are but partially utilized. Never was a field for both capital and labor more inviting. The resources of Georgia have only to be known to attract to her the idle capital of other countries as well as our own, and an industrious population to utilize it in almost every known branch of human industry.

Animated by these considerations, although it may not be expressly laid down in the catalogue of my official duties contained in the law creating the Department of Agriculture of the State of Georgia, as Commissioner and executive head of that Department, I feel it to be due to my State that this *desideratum*, the absence of which is operating so injuriously to her best interest and progress, should be supplied, and perhaps, by no one more appropriately than myself. The representations of parties personally interested are always regarded with more or less distrust; while an official statement of facts, obtained from sources known to be trustworthy, by a sworn, responsibible officer of the government, is entitled to, and will generally command, the attention and confidence of the public.

In the preparation of this Manual— the object of which is to show the superior advantages which Georgia offers to the capitalist and the immigrant, I have sought to avoid all exaggeration, and to exclude everything that was even doubtful. I have, therefore, confined its statements to *facts*, such as every intelligent and well-informed citizen of the State will be willing to vouch for. If the picture is not more glowing, it is simply because I am determined that no one shall be misled by its statements.

With this introduction, which is necessary to a correct understanding of the object in view in the preparation of the work, I proceed to consider the State of Georgia in the various aspects in which it is likely to interest the public, and especially the several classes to which reference has been made. And, that the exposition may not be tiresome, the utmost brevity is promised.

PART I.

GEOGRAPHICAL SITUATION OF GEORGIA.

The State of Georgia lies in the southeastern portion of the United States, and, with Florida, constitutes the extreme portion of the American Union in that direction. In the original settlement, its chartered limits extended from the Atlantic ocean to the Mississippi river, with the 35th parallel of north latitutude as its northern boundary, and the 31st parallel and Florida as its boundary on the South. Early in the present century, a very large portion of this territory westward—nearly two-thirds—was ceded to the United States, and out of it, in great part, have since been formed the two new States of Alabama and Mississippi.

From the above, it will be seen that the entire State lies within the southern portion of the Temperate zone, and, as a consequence, is exempt, alike, from the rigors and other discomforts and disadvantages of a cold climate and the debility and diseases incident to tropical regions. It may be said, with perfect truth, that there is no part of the known world where a greater degree of physical comfort can be secured the year round, or where a greater amount of labor can be performed in the usual vocations within the same period of time, than in Georgia. But these points will be more fully treated under their appropriate heads.

The geographical situation of Georgia is worthy of note in another, the commercial view, of the question. The 32d parallel of north latitude passes nearly through the centre of the State ; the great southern trans-continental line of railway, to connect the Atlantic and Pacific oceans by a communication uninterrupted by snows in winter, and open the year round, has been located on and near that parallel. Savannah, Georgia's principal seaport, is but 15′ north of that line, and is destined to become the eastern terminus of this great highway of trade. It is 943 miles nearer to San Diego, on the California coast, than New York—the eastern terminus of the northern lines—is to San Francisco ; the distance between the two latter cities being 3,456 miles, while the distance between the two former is only 2,512 miles. This road will be completed in a very few years, and its beneficial effects upon the trade and general prosperity of Georgia are too obvious to require comment. The facts stated show that this southern line is destined to become the favorite highway of the Pacific trade, including that of China and Japan, with the ports of Georgia as its chief *entrepots* in the East.

Georgia, from her geographical relations, is also the natural highway to the teeming products of the great agricultural heart of the country—the Mississippi Valley. A straight line from St. Louis, or the mouth of the Ohio, shows that the Atlantic coast of Georgia is much nearer and more accessible to the commerce of the West than that of any other State in the Union. Several lines of railway between these two sections are already in successful operation; while a projected canal from the Tennessee river to the head of navigation on the Altamaha tributaries in Georgia, will afford ample water transportation to the commerce of the West seeking European markets, and, in point of time, speedier than that hitherto employed—the circuitous route *via* the Mississippi river and the Gulf of Mexico. This canal route has been surveyed by direction of Congress, its practicability and cheapness fully determined, and its construction made a simple question of time.

TERRITORIAL EXTENT AND CAPACITY FOR POPULATION.

Georgia is ample in her domain. The State has an average length (north and south) of about 300 miles, and an average breadth (east and west) of about 200 miles, and is, with the exception of Florida, the largest of the American States east of the Mississippi River. The superficial area is 58,000 square miles, or, by land measurement, 37,120,000 acres. Nearly the whole of this vast surface is susceptible of profitable tillage; those portions that are too mountainous, and the irreclaimable swamps, including the salt marshes along the coast, being estimated at only about *one* per cent. There is no sterile land in Georgia, and it may be safely said that no portion of the globe of equal extent is capable of producing more to satisfy the wants of man.

We have seen that the State has an area of 58,000 square miles. Her population, according to the last census, taken in 1870, was, in round numbers, 1,184,000, or a fraction over 20 to the square mile. Allowing her producing capacity to be only equal to that of other nations, we may form some idea of the additional population she is capable of sustaining, by a comparison of the above figures with those of other countries. As we only wish to illustrate, we shall name but a few that are well known to the civilized world:

England, with an area of 50,300 square miles, or less than that of Georgia by nearly 8,000, supports a population of 21,290,000, or over nineteen times greater than that of Georgia.

Ireland, with an area of 32,530 square miles, being a little over half the size of Georgia, sustains a population of 5,412,000, or nearly five times greater than that of Georgia.

Norway and Sweden, with an area of 294,000 square miles, or about five times that of Georgia, have about the same population to the square mile, with, perhaps, not one tenth the same productive capacity.

France, with an area of 204,000 square miles, or less than four times as great as that of Georgia, supports a population of 36,103,-000, or over thirty times as great as that of Georgia.

Holland, with an area of 12,700 square miles, or a little more than one-fifth that of Georgia, supports a population of 3,810,000, or over three times that of Georgia.

Belgium, with an area of 11,370 square miles, or less than one-fifth that of Georgia, supports a population of 5,337,000, or nearly five times that of Georgia.

Switzerland, with an area of 15,990 square miles, mostly mountainous, or about three and a half times less than that of Georgia, has a population of 2,650,000, or over double that of Georgia.

Prussia, with an area of 136,100 square miles, or about two and a third times greater than that of Georgia, sustains a population of 25,773,000, or about twenty-five times that of Georgia.

These comparisons—in some instances with countries whose climates and topographical conditions are unfavorable to production, as for instance, Switzerland, and Norway and Sweden—will serve to show the vast reserved capabilities of Georgia, and what immense additions might be made to her present population without crowding to an extent where subsistence would be insufficient, or even difficult.

FACE OF THE COUNTRY.

The nominal divisions of the State are three-fold, to-wit : Lower, Middle, and Upper Georgia. These correspond, in the order stated, with the three great natural divisions, viz : the low country, the Hill country and the mountain region.

Lower Georgia lies below the line crossing the heads of navigation of the rivers, a portion of which flow into the Atlantic Ocean, and a portion into the Gulf of Mexico. It is the largest of the three divisions, comprising about 35,000 square miles. It lies, for the most part, below the level of 300 feet above the sea, the average elevation being about 250 feet.

Middle Georgia lies between the heads of navigation and the elevation of 1,000 or 1,100 feet, the average being 750 feet. It has an area of 15,000 square miles.

Upper Georgia constitutes the northern portion of the State, and embraces all the mountains of any note, and much hill country. It has an area of about 10,000 square miles. The eastern half has an average elevation of about 1,500 feet, whilst there are mountain chains that rise to the height of 3,000 feet, and peaks to 4,800 feet. The western half is much lower, the general elevation being only 750 feet, with mountains up to 2,000 feet.

The average elevation of the surface of the State is 650 feet above the sea.

These three divisions of the State differ in soil and climate, and, to some extent, in productions, as we shall have occasion to note more particularly hereafter, when we come to treat of those several topics.

The mountains of Georgia constitute the southern terminus of the great Appalachian chain, which, commencing at the mouth of the St. Lawrence, in the north, traverses that portion of America lying east of the Mississippi river, conforming in general direction to the line of coast, until it finally loses itself in Georgia and Alabama, in the south. Its highest points are at either extremity, some of the peaks in Georgia, as already stated, rising to an elevation of near 5,000 feet above the level of the sea. Connected with this chain are the great ridges, or water-sheds, which divide the waters of the Atlantic from those of the Gulf of Mexico. The chief of these water-sheds, in this section of the country, is the Chattahoochee ridge, which enters Georgia in the northeast from North Carolina, and, after passing through the State, nearly dividing it equally, extends to the capes of Florida. On the east of this great ridge lies the Atlantic slope of Georgia, comprising about 30,000 square miles; on the west, the Gulf slope, with an area of about 28,000 square miles.

Though mountainous, this Northern or Upper Georgia division is interspersed with rich valleys and hill country, susceptible of cultivation.

Middle Georgia is undulating throughout, without mountains, or level plains to any great extent, and is a very productive portion of the State. With the exception of a narrow belt on the coast, it has been the longest settled. Nearly every acre of it is susceptible of cultivation, the only exception being the swamps that border some of the water-courses, nearly all of which, however, can be reclaimed and made productive.

The remaining division, or Lower Georgia, is, for the most part, a level country, the soil generally light and sandy, and the natural growth, especially of the uplands, is pine. It is said to be the finest timber country on the continent. The yellow, or longleaf pine still abounds, as it is the least cleared portion of the State; and the rivers and railroads furnish convenient and cheap modes of transportating it to market. The lands remote from the water-courses, though generally not very fertile, are still valuable for agricultural purposes, and susceptible, perhaps, of a greater variety of productions than any other division of the State. Much of this pine land is hilly, and the residents in such localities—which almost invariably border the flat lands—have good water and enjoy good health throughout the year.

Georgia has a sea-front of about 200 miles, indented with some of the finest harbors on the Atlantic coast. Savannah, Darien, Brunswick and St. Mary's are her principal sea-ports, all of which can communicate by inland navigation through channels running inside of a chain of islands which line the coast throughout its enire length.

In nothing regarding us, is a greater mistake made abroad, and indeed, in some parts of our own country, than in the climate, or atmospheric conditions, of Georgia. The State being in the southern portion of the Union, lying between parallels of latitude 30°, 39′, 27″ (average) and 35°, the stranger naturally concludes that our climate is mild and delightful in winter; and in this he is correct. We have but little snow—in more than half the State none at all for years together—we import or manufacture all our ice, and field work may be kept up at all periods of the year. The difficulty with strangers is in determining the character of our climate during the summer months. The winters being pleasant and genial, they conclude, without further investigation, that the summers must necessarily be hot and sultry. This is a serious mistake, as all will testify who have any practical knowledge of the subject. No finer summer climate is to be found on the continent, east of the Mississippi river, than that of many parts of Georgia, and, as a whole, it will compare favorably in this respect with that of the States of the north and northwest. Carefully conducted observations, year after year, show that the mean annual temperature of the city of Atlanta, our State Capital, is the same with that of Washington City, Louisville, Kentucky, and St. Louis, in the State of Missouri, which are from 800 to 880 miles further north. The mean annual temperature south of a line drawn across the State from Augusta to Columbus, is between 64° and 68°; between the same line and another parallel to it, and running twenty miles south of Atlanta, we have a mean annual temperature between 60° and 64°; in another strip of territory including Atlanta, we have a mean temperature the year round of between 56° and 60°. In what we have described as Upper Georgia, it is between 52° and 56°, while in the mountains it is below 52°. The mean of Gainesville, in Hall county, and of Clarksville and Mount Airy, in Habersham county, corresponds with that of Central Ohio, Indiana, Illinois, Upper Missouri and Lower Nebraska. We refer to the map of the State for a better understanding of the several localities above referred to, as well as the significance of the figures given in this connection. We have the winter climate of Rome, and the summer climate of Jerusalem.

In explanation of these facts, certain features in the geographical situation and physical conformation of the State must be taken into consideration. In Lower Georgia we find the greatest degree of heat in summer, the mercury sometimes rising as high as 96°, rarely above that figure. It lies, however, between the Atlantic Ocean and the Gulf of Merico, in close proximity to both, and the temperature is greatly modified by the strong currents of sea air which continually pass from one of these great bodies of water to the other. The mean temperature of Savannah, in the southeastern portion of the State, during the months of June, July and August, is 79° to 80°; and in no part of Southern Georgia does the mercury often rise above 90°, whilst in winter it seldom descends to the freezing point. Sun-strokes, so common in the Northern and Northwestern States, are almost wholly unknown in Georgia.

Elevation affects temperture, on an average, 1° Fahrenheit for every 300 feet. This, alone, would make a difference in Georgia of 16° by reason of relative elevation between the shore level and the highest summit. It is also affected by latitude, and there being a difference of about 4½° between the northern and the southern limits of the State, the thermometer should show a difference of about 9° in the temperature.

But latitude, without the aid of elevation, may not always materially affect temperature. There are other natural causes that may antagonize its influence The difference in the length of the days may increase the summer range in more northern latitudes. At New York, for instance, in mid summer the days are nearly an hour longer than they are at Savannah, and at Quebec, in Canada, nearly one hour and a half longer, and the nights correspondingly shorter; the consequence is, at New York there is one hour longer for the heat to accumulate from the direct rays of the sun, and one hour less time in the night for the heat thus accumulated to be carried off by radiation. This is said to be the cause why northern latitudes are hotter in summer than southern latitudes.

Finally, we have no hesitation in saying that, take it the year round, the climate of Georgia is equal to any to be found on the globe, whether we regard personal comfort in in-door and in out-door work, or the production of crops for the support of man and beast, both in the summer and the winter months. We may mention a fact in this connection : The city of Atlanta is situated within a few miles of the southern line of what is called Northern or Upper Georgia, which contains the mountainous region, and yet we know many farmers in the immediate vicinity who have pastured their stock throughout the past winter, and kept them in excellent condition on the growing crops of wheat, rye and barley.

RAINFALL.

The amount of annual rainfall in Georgia varies in different sections of the State, and also according to locality in the several sections. It is greatest on the sea-coast, and, as a general rule, diminishes as you advance toward the northern border. The average quantity at Savannah is about 57 inches, and the general average in the State is from 46 to 50 inches, or about 5,000 tons weight to the acre. The distribution of this amount of water—a most important consideration—is such as to secure a fair general average of crops. There are no periodical wet and dry seasons. Irrigation on a large scale is wholly unknown in Georgia, except on the rice plantations, where occasional flows of water facilitate successful cultivation. Crops are sometimes cut short in some localities from the want of a proper amount of moisture ; but we have never known a total failure of the crops from drought, or from any other cause, in Georgia.

SOILS AND PRODUCTIONS.

The soils of Georgia are among the very best of the older States; in virgin fertility she surpassed them all, as is evidenced by her rapid settlement from other States upon the extinguishment of the Indian title to the lands. Injudicious cultivation, in the haste to get rich, has done much, in past years, to impair and waste their strength ; but wiser views are now obtaining, and with systems of culture greatly improved, production is steadily increasing without material addition to the population

The soils of Georgia are as various as the elements of rocks and vegetable and animal remains that compose them.

In Upper Georgia, or the northern-most division of the State, the soil is a mixture of clay and sand. In the western half of this section, there is a large admixture of lime. and the clay is generally red, with here and there a yellowish brown or drab. In the eastern half, the clay is altogether reddish, and the soil not calcareous. The valley and coves of both are very rich and productive, while the hill-sides yield generously to judicious cultivation. There are many fine farms on the very summit of the Blue Ridge and Lookout range of mountains.

The chief agricultural productions of Upper Georgia are Indian corn or maize, wheat, barley, rye, oats, potatoes, sorghum. and all the grasses, including clover. Its wheat, with that of Middle Georgia, is considered the heaviest and best grown in the Union, and always commands a premium in the Northern markets. All the grains mentioned grow to great perfection, and the yield of hay, where proper attention is given that crop, is very large. The soil and climate are also admirably adapted to tobacco, though it has no', up to this time, received that attention as a crop that it deserves. Many good judges consider Upper Georgia, in this respect, superior to either Virginia or North Carolina, as the soil is not only su.table, but the season for planting is much earlier, and of growth longer, enabling the farmer to gather a second crop from the same plants. Until a very recent date, this section of the State was regarded as unsuited to the successful cultivation of cotton, but the introduation of commercial fertilizers, the effect of which is to hasten growth and maturity and increase production, has brought about quite a revolution as regards the great staple. It is now being successfully grown, in considerable quantities, as far north as the Tennessee line. As evidence of the rapid increase in the production of cotton in this section, we may mention the fact that the city of Atlanta, whose trade in that commodity ten years ago was so inconsiderable as scarcely to have a place in the local market reports, had received, up to the first of April of the present year (1878), or in seven out of the twelve cotton months, 98,000 bales, grown almost exclusively in Upper Georgia. Hemp, flax and jute may also be grown with profit. During a good part of the year, the mountains afford the finest range for cattle, sheep and goats, whilst hogs keep fat in the fall and early winter months on the masts of nuts and acorns. All the varieties of vegetables flourish in this part of the State. The fruits that thrive best are the apple, the pear, the cherry, the plum and the grape; also the raspberry and strawberry. The last mentioned, may be said to grow equally well in every part of the State. The spring and well water of this section is unsurpassed in any part of the world.

The surface of Middle Georgia is rolling, and the soil generally red, with here and there a liberal admixture of gray, and very strong and productive. All things considered, this is regarded as the most desirable portion of the State, if not ot the South. It is the great cotton section, or the section where the soil will yield a greater amount of fruit than a like area of equal fertility, in any other part of the State. Indian corn, wheat, barley, rye—indeed, all the cereal crops—are cultivated, and yield in their greatest abundance. Even the oldest lands of this section recuperate rapidly under good treatment, and are soon restored to their original fertility. Improved systems of culture are obtaining very generally throughout this part of the State, which is the most populous of the three great divisions, and, as a consequense, production is progressive. Of fruits, the apple, pear, peach, fig, grape, melons, and indeed every variety, other than tropical, are grown with the greatest success. The finest peaches in the world grow in this section and in the northern portion of Lower Georgia, and large quantities are shipped annually to the northern cities. Melons, also, are grown to great perfection, and constitute quite important item of the commerce of this section. The forests and abandoned fields abound in nuts and berries in large variety, furnished by nature without care or cultivation. Dried fruits are becoming an important item in the exports from this section.

It may be said with truth that no country in the world offers greater natural advantages than this middle section of Georgia. Embracing a territory about two hundred miles in length from east to west, and one hundred broad from north to south, intersected by numerous rivers and smaller water courses, the amount of water power available for manufacturing purposes is incalculable. It constitutes the heart of the cotton region, and the material is consequently at hand to be worked into the various fabrics. Ten railroads cross it in various directions, so that transportation is all that could be desired. Its drinking water is excellent, and its health unterrupted throughout the year.

Southern, or Lower Georgia, consists chiefly of sandy, pine land, with occasional belts of oak and hickory, and where these occur the soil has a considerable mixture of reddish or light-brown clay, and is very productive. The lands generally are light and easy of cultivation, and while some portions, especially those on the water courses of the southwest and the red lands above referred to, are very rich, nearly the whole is tillable, and with occasional light manuring, continue to produce good crops from year to year. It is, as a general rule, sparsely settled, and the lands are the cheapest in the State. The leading field products are cotton, sugar cane, corn, rice, oats, potatoes and field peas. The country being open, and the pasturage good throughout the year, large numbers of beef cattle and sheep are raised annually for market, at a cost purely nominal, as they require neither to be fed nor sheltered. Wool forms quite an item in the list of its exports; near 75,000 pounds were cleared at the custom-house at Brunswick alone during the past year.

Cotton is produced generally throughout the section, the sea-island or long staple variety in the counties bordering on Florida and along the coast. This class of cotton is used in the manufacture of the finer fabrics, and in combination with silk, but is less cultivated than in former years, the demand for it having been lessened by the improvement in the staple and quality of the common cotton, and in the machinery for its manufacture.

The cotton crop of Georgia averages a little over 500,000 bales, or about 225,000,000 pounds, worth, at ten cents per pound, $22,500,000.

The rice lands lie chiefly on tide water, and are among the most valuable and productive on the southern coast. Considerable rice is also grown, chiefly for home consumption, on inland swamps and low lands in Middle as well as in Lower Georgia, though the rice that enters into commerce comes chiefly from the country along the coast.

Sugar cane is also an important crop of Southern Georgia, and could be made among the most profitable. It grows luxuriantly, and yields profitable returns in sugar and syrup. Yet, but little sugar is made for market, the planters usually confining themselves to a sufficiency for home demand, and relying chiefly upon the syrup as a marketable crop. To show the capacity of the soil under high culture, we mention one instance among the many of equal production that are well vouched for. In 1874, Mr. John J. Parker, of Thomas county, produced, on one acre, 694½ gallons of cane syrup, worth seventy-five cents per gallon, or $520.87. The total cost of production was $77.50, leaving a net profit of $443.37.

This section of the State also produces an excellent quality of light tobacco, such as is manufactured into cigars, though the plant will eventually run into the heavy leaf unless the seed are renewed annually from the West Indies.

Notwithstanding the variety of soils and climates, vegetables of every description do well in all parts of the State; but it is chiefly in the section along the coast that they are raised for distant markets. Most of the varieties maturing here in early spring, before the seeds are planted in the Northern States of the Union, they command a good price in consequence, and the producers realize handsomely from their business. In the spring of 1877, there were shipped to the Northern markets, from the port of Savannah alone, 23,284 packages of fruit, 20,405 packages of vegetables and 26,345 melons.

Of the fruits of this section, melons, strawberries, grapes and some oranges are those chiefly cultivated for market. The fig and grape grow to great perfection, and the orange, lemon, lime, banana, pomegranate, of the tropical fruits, succeed well where attention has been given to their cultivation. Some varieties of the pear also thrive well in this section of the State. The Scuppernong grape grows in its greatest perfection; the crops are very heavy and the fruit sweeter than that grown in more northern latitudes.

Lower Georgia is said to resemble, in soil and climate, those portions of Prussia that lie in the vicinity of the capital. The soil is, however, in its natural state, far more productive, and consequently requires less labor and expense to be kept in good planting condition. Although generally sandy, it has a good clay foundation, or subsoil, from six to twelve inches below the surface, which enables it to retain fertilizers and hold them as plant food.

CAPACITY OF GEORGIA SOIL UNDER HIGH CULTURE.

The various agricultural products common to Georgia having been given with some minuteness in the chapter on Soils and Productions, we proceed to give the results of a number of experiments in the cultivation of those products, in each of those disvisions, conducted with proper preparation and fertilization—such as are given in the more densely settled portions of the world. As but little is accomplished by inadequate means in any department of human industry, the actual producing capacity of a country can only be tested by the results of *judicious* culture. The crops, to which we shall refer, were reported to the various State and county fairs within the past few years, and both the culture and its results were verified by the affidavits of disinterested parties.

In 1873, Mr. R. H. Hardaway produced, on upland, in Thomas county, (Lower Georgia) 119 bushels of Indian corn, or maize, on one acre, which yielded a net profit of $77 17.

In the same county, the same year, Mr. E. T. Davis produced 96½ bushels of rust-proof oats per acre. After the oats were harvested, he planted the same land in cotton, and in the fall gathered 800 pounds of seed cotton.

Mr. John J. Parker, of the same county, produced, in 1874, on one acre, 694½ gallons of cane syrup, at a cost of $77.50. The syrup, at 75 cents per gallon, the market price, brought $520.87—net profit from one acre, $443 37.

In 1874, Mr. Wiley W. Groover, of Brooks county, (Lower Georgia) produced, with two horses, on a farm of 126½ acres, without the aid of commercial fertilizers, cotton, corn, oats, peas, sugar cane and potatoes, to the value of $3,258.25. The total cost of production was $1,045.00, leaving net proceeds of crop, $2,213.25. The stock raised on the farm was not counted.

Joseph Hodges, of the same county, produced, on one acre, 2,700 pounds of seed cotton; Wm. Borden, 600 gallons of syrup; J. Bower, 500 bushels of sweet potatoes; J. O. Morton, 75 bushels oats. Mr. T. W. Jones made 12 barrels, or 480 gallons, of syrup on one acre, and saved enough cane for seed.

In Bulloch county, (Lower Georgia) 3,500 pounds seed cotton were produced by Samuel Groover, and in the same county 21 barrels surgar at one time, and 700 gallons syrup at another, per acre.

In Clay county, Mr. —— Hodge produced from one acre, a few years ago, 4,500 pounds of seed cotton.

Mr. J. R. Respass, of Schley county, gathered the present year (1878) a little upwards of 500 bushels of oats from five acres.

Mr. J. R. Respass, of Schley county, (Lower Georgia) in 1877, by the use of fertilizers, grew on five acres of naturally poor land, 15,000 pounds of seed cotton, which netted him when sold $66.02 per acre.

Mr. H. T. Peeples, of Berrien county, reports to this Department a crop of 800 bushels of sweet potatoes grown on one acre of pine land.

In 1876, Mr. G. J. Drake, of Spalding county, (Middle Georgia) produced 74 bushels of corn on one acre of land.

Mr. John Bonner, of Carroll county, made three bales of cotton (500 pounds each) on one acre. Mr. R. H. Springer, of the same county, produced nine bales from five acres, without manures, and ninety-four bales from 100 acres, by the use of fertilizers.

In 1873, Mr. S. W. Leak, of the same county, produced on one acre 40¼ bushels of wheat, worth $80.50; cost $14.50—net profit $66.

In Wilkes county 123 bushels corn was produced on one acre of bottom land; also 42 bushels Irish potatoes on one-tenth acre, the second crop same year on same land; the first crop very fine, but not so good.

Mr. J. F. Madden, of the same county, produced, in 1876, on one acre, 137 bushels of oats.

Mr. T. C. Warthen, of Washington county, (on the line of Middle and Lower Georgia) produced, in 1873, on 1.1125 acres, 6,917 pounds of seed cotton, equivalent to five bales of 461 pounds each, worth, at 17½ cents per pound—the average price of that year—403.37. The cost of culture was $148.58; net profit, $254.79, for a very small fraction over one acre.

Dr. Wm. Jones, of Burke county, produced 480 gallons syrup on one acre. Wesley Jones, of the same county, produced three bales of cotton, 500 pounds each, per acre. Jas. J. Davis, in same county, made, in 1877, with two mules, thirty-four bales of cotton, 500 pounds each, 600 bushels corn, and 300 bushels oats. Wm. C. Palmer, of same county, made, in 1877, with one mule, twenty-five bales of cotton, 500 pounds each, and a fair crop of corn. Henry Miller, of same county, produced, in 1877, sixty-five bushels corn per acre, first year, on reclaimed swamp, without manures.

Mr. R. M. Brooks, of Pike county, (Middle Georgia) produced, in 1873, on five acres of bottom land, 500 bushels of rice. The total cost was $75—net profit, $300.

Mr. R. B. Baxter, of Hancock county, (Middle Georgia) in 1872, harvested at the first cutting, first year's crop, 4,862 pounds of dry clover hay per acre.

Mr. A. J. Preston, of Crawford county, gathered, from one acre of Flint river bottom, 4,000 pounds seed cotton, and from another, on same place, 115 bushels corn.

Dr. T. P. Janes, of Greene county, (Middle Georgia) produced, in 1871, five tons of clover hay per acre, in one season, at two cuttings.

Mr. Patrick Long, of Bibb county, (on the line of Middle and Lower Georgia) harvested from one acre of land, from which he had gathered a crop of cabbages in June of the same year, 8,646 pounds of native crab-grass hay.

Mr. S. W. Leak, in Spalding county, (Middle Georgia) gathered, in the fall of 1873, from one acre, from which he had harvested forty bushels of wheat in June, 10,726 pounds of pea-vine hay. Net profit from wheat, $66; from pea-vine hay, $233.08, making, in one year from a single acre, a net profit of $299.08.

Mr. William Smith, of Coweta county, (Middle Georgia) produced 2,200 pounds seed cotton per acre on ten acres.

Mr. Edward Camp, of the same county, produced 1,000 bushels oats from ten acres.

Mr. J. T. Manley, of Spalding county, (Middle Georgia) produced 115 bushels of oats from one acre.

Mr. S. W. Bloodworth, of the same county, gathered, in 1870, 137 bushels of corn from one acre.

Mr. L. B. Willis, in Greene county, (Middle Georgia) in June, 1873, from one acre and a third, harvested twenty bushels of wheat, and the following October, 27,130 pounds of corn forage. From the forage alone he received a profit of $159.22 per acre.

Dr. W. Moody, of the same county, harvested, at one cutting, from one acre of river bottom, in 1874, 13,953 pounds of Bermuda grass hay; cost, $12.87, value of hay, $209 29, net profit, $196.42.

Mr. J. R Winters, of Cobb county, (Upper Georgia) produced, in 1873, from 1.15 acres, 6,575 pounds of dry clover hay at the first cutting of the second year's crop.

Mr. T. H. Moore, of same county, produced on one acre 105 bushels of corn, while Mr. Jeremiah Daniel produced 125 bushels.

Mr. R. Peters, Jr., of Gordon county, (Upper Georgia) harvested, in 1874, from three acres of lucerne, four years old, fourteen tons and 200 pounds of hay, or 9,400 pounds per acre.

Capt. C. W. Howard produced, on Lookout Mountain, in Walker county (Upper Georgia), in 1874, on one acre of unmanured land, which cost him twenty-five cents per acre, with one hoeing and plowing, 108½ bushels of Irish potatoes, which he sold in Atlanta at a net profit of $97.25. On land manured and better prepared and worked, double that quantity could be produced.

Mr. Thomas Smith, of Cherokee county, produced 104 bushels of corn from one acre.

Mr. John Dyer, of Bibb county, produced, in 1873, from one acre, at a cost of $8.00, 398.7 bushels of sweet potatoes, which he sold at a net profit of $290.92.

Mr. Haddon P. Redding, of Fulton county, in 1877, produced from one acre 400 bushels of St. Domingo yam potatoes, which he readily sold in Atlanta at an average price of $1.00 per bushel.

These instances of production are exceptional, and far beyond the usual results of farming in our State; but they serve to show the capacity of our soil when properly fertilized, and cultivated with intelligence under the guidance of science. It will not be denied, however, that what the parties named have accomplished on a limited scale, may be done by others on still larger areas, and with corresponing results.

TIMBER.

The varied natural forest growth of Georgia is capable of furnishing woods ample for all purposes. Our Geological cabinet contains specimens of 130 varieties, and there are 100 others not embraced in the collection. In the Northern division of the State, we have cedar, poplar, hickory, beech, maple, chestnut, white, red, black and post oaks; white, spruce, and short-leaf pine; the latter ample for all demands of builders. In the Middle division we have nearly all of the above-mentioned, with the addition of walnut, cherry, china, elm, and ash, all of which are valuable for mechanical uses. In the Southern division, besides some of those already enumerated, the long-leaf or yellow pine, the great tree of commerce, abounds. For building and ship timber, this wood stands without a rival in the markets of the world, and the supply would seem to be inexhaustible. The section under consideration embraces about 30,000 square miles, 24,000 of which our State Geologist, who has special charge of that interest, estimates is uncleared, and will produce, on an average, 30,000 feet of first-class heart timber per acre. Nor does its uses stop here. From the pine is extracted the turpentine, rosin, tar and pitch of commerce, and vast fields of it are devoted to that purpose. The curled pine of the coast country, in beauty and susceptibility of polish, is without a rival among the woods of any part of the world. For panel-work, and furniture of all kinds, it is admirably adapted. Specimens of this cabinet variety of the pine have been sent to the Paris Exposition of 1878, and visitors curious in such matters are invited to inspect it. The live-oak, remarkable for its weight and toughness, and so largely used in the construction of those parts of ships that are subject to the greatest strain, is found in large quantities along the whole line of the Georgia coast, and on the sea-islands. In the same localities, we have the bay and the cedar, also useful for manufacturing purposes. In the river bottoms and swamps of the entire lower half of the State, the cypress growes to an immense size, and without limit as to quantity. This is also a most durable wood, though soft in texture, and easily worked. For shingles, weather-boarding, wood-ware, ship sides fence posts, indeed for most purposes where exposure to the weather is necessary, there are few woods that will answer a better purpose or last longer. Our river bottoms all over the State are well supplied with white-oak, which, for carriage and wagon timber, and for barrel staves, is considered superior to all other woods. Ash, also used largely in carriage factories, abounds in the same localities.

These are but a few of the many woods of the State which might
be mentioned as both usefnl or ornamental. Of the supply, it need
only be said that full 60 per cent., at least, of the original forest
growth, or 22,200,000 out of the 37,000,000 acres, is still standing,
which, with the immense beds of coal for fuel, will be found ample
for all the wants of the State for hundreds of years to come. Timber and sawed lumber, including staves and shingles, constitute a
very important item of Georgia's foreign and coastwise trade.
Complete statistics of this trade for the year 1877—one of great
depression in this as well as other interests—have not yet come to
hand. It aggregates many millions of dollars, and with the exception stated, has been steadily increasing from year to year. We
annex a statement of the shipments for last year from the four
leading ports of the State. There are other points of shipment, and
much of the lumber of the southwestern portion of the State finds
an outlet through the ports of Florida :

TIMBER AND LUMBER EXPORTS, 1877.

Savannah, superficial feet		51,281,972
Darien, " "		74,106,152
St. Mary's " "		18,116,000
Brunswick " "		19,092,410
Total		162,596,534

METALS AND MINERALS OF GEORGIA.

It is conceded by all who have any adequate information on the
subject, that the mineral resources of Georgia, in extent and value,
are unsurpassed, if equalled, by those of any other American State.
The variety and richness of her ores, and other natural products
of a kindred nature, are facts which, in their full force, have lain
buried beneath the earth's surface until recent scientific explora-
tions, under the direction of the State Government, brought them
to the light. It being impossible without too great elaboration, to
go through the long catalogue of specimens that lie exposed to
view on the shelves of our Geological Museum, we shall confine
our observations to a few leading products, which will fully establish the position that, to the miner, no country on the globe
presents advantages superior to those of Georgia.

GOLD.—It is impossible to estimate the true value of this interest, and all calculations must be based upon the actual production
of the mines in the past, and indications of the presence of that
precious metal as they appear to the scientific eye. These are the
only reliable data, and we shall limit our remarks to what they
will fully justify.

Dr. George Little, State Geologist, after a thorough exploration
of the auriferous region, declares as his conviction, that, *all things*

considered, Georgia, as a gold-mining region, offers inducements equal to those of California. We quote his remarks on this point, as they are both full and interesting. He says:

" But you must remember that this is not the best point that is offered by our North Georgia mines. You see it is not the quantity of gold that makes a section valuable to miners. It is the facility with which the ore is mined; it is the ease with which it can be sent to market; it is the cheapness of labor; it is the nearness of timber and water courses; it is the healthfulness of the climate and the facility with which provisions may be procured. In all these points Georgia excels. A ton of ore in the Black Hills, of twice the richness, is not worth as much as a ton of ore in Georgia. A mine of enormous richness is of little value if it is in the heart of an impenetrable or dangerous or malarious region. Lumps of gold might exist at the north pole without being of any practical value. There are scientists who believe that great masses of this precious metal are to be found at the centre of the earth. Of what account is it, however, to us?

" Now, the gold of North Georgia is in a perfectly accessible region. It is penetrated by first class railways, and by short and reliable hack lines. Every part of it is civilized, and convenient to cities. And, better than all, the gold lies near to the surface, and is easily reached by the miner. The timber needed to run the furnaces is right at hand, and procurable cheap. The climate is the best in the world, and is a famous resort for invalids. The watercourses that pour down the hills give the best possible power. It is necessary to transport only a short distance, while in California it is frequently carried fifty and one hundred miles. Labor is cheap and easily procurable. In fact, all the elements of cheap working for gold appear to be united in this section.

"The greatest advantage, however, is in the fact that most of the ore in North Georgia is partially decomposed, and is worked with great facility. Where you would have to blast the quartz in California, you can work it with a pick, or even a shovel. Consequently, ore that is much poorer than the California ore can be mined here at a profit, while there it would involve a loss. It does look as if nature had conspired to put the enormous amount of gold in North Georgia in the hands of the miner.

" Besides the above advantages, it is very rich—as rich as any ore to be found anywhere."

Such is the testimony of an intelligent and disinterested officer of the government, who owns not a foot of our gold territory, nor a share in our mines.

The gold belt of Georgia is about one hundred miles in breadth, with barren intervals here and there. It lies northeast and southwest across the entire northern and part of the eastern section of

the State, and loses itself in the eastern portion of Alabama.   It
extends through a large number of counties.   It has been found as
low as Columbia county, in the eastern portion of Middle Georgia,
and as far north and west as Fannin county, which borders on the
State of Tennessee.   But few mines have been developed in Columbia and Lincoln counties, but they are claimed to be among the
richest in the State.   A vein near Goshen, in the latter county, is
said to be yielding at the present time, $1,000 per month at a cost
of but, $115.   That portion of intermediate territory which is
barren of gold, is comparatively small, being much less than
one-half of the whole.   While many very rich and profitable
mines have been opened in the lower portion of the belt, the
greater proportion of the mining has been done in the northern or
mountainous section, especially in the counties of Lumpkin,
White, Union, Dawson and Cherokee.

The gold occurs under three distinct conditions : First, as sand
(dust), or pebbles (nuggets), forming integral portions of the deposits of sand and gravel along the streams, which sometimes extend as high as 100 feet or more, above the stream levels.   Second:
as grains, strings, or masses, forming integral portions of extensive beds of schists, which are sometimes accompanied by layers
of quartz of greater or less thickness, and are sometimes destitute
of the least particle of quartz.   Third : as a part or the whole, of
the mineral contents of quartz veins.

Much the greater portion of the gold heretofore mined in
Georgia has been obtained from the stream deposits, and by rude
methods, such as washing in sluices, rockers, and toms, from
which a very large proportion of the smaller particles escape.   In
this rough way, from $1.00 to $2.00 per day is usually obtained to
the hand, though many deposits have been worked which yielded
as much as $3.00 and $5.00 per hand.   The quartz veins vary in
thickness from a few inches to ten feet, or more, and have seldom
been worked below the water level, from want of capital to purchase the necessary machinery.   The ore, when obtained from
the veins, is pounded in mills run by water-power, and the yield
generally varies from $5,00 to $50.00 per ton, the cost of handling
being about 50 cents per ton.   There are, however, many instances
where the yield has been as high as $60.00, and even as high as
$100 00 per ton.   The business is making steady progress in all the
mining districts, and we have returns to date of 34 mills with 337
stamps now in operation, though there are doubtless others not
yet brought to our knowledge.   The stamps are of hardened iron,
and in weight range from 350 to 750 pounds.   They reduce, each,
from one to two tons per day of twelve hours, the quantity depending upon the weight of the stamp and the hardness of the
ore.   These mills are located chiefly in Lumpkin and White
counties.

During the last few years there has been quite a revival in the business of gold-mining. Large amounts of northern capital have been attracted to Georgia, and there has been great progress both in the quantity and quality of the machinery used for that purpose. The chief agency in giving this new impulse to the gold interest, is what is known as the *Hand Canal*, in Lumpkin county, the heart of the gold region. Its purpose is to utilize the splendid water power of that section in the business of mining, and vast sums have been expended on the work already. This canal has opened up a new era in gold-digging. Wherever available, it dispenses, in a great measure, with expensive transportation, with steam machinery in the mines and for elevating the ore, and reduces the amount of labor necessary for the attainment of given results fully one-half, if not more. In addition to this, it renders mining operations exhaustive; under the action of so searching an agent, the earth is compelled to yield up all its treasures, no matter how carefully they may have been hidden away from human sight. A brief description of this canal is necessary for a proper understanding of the operations for gold in that immediate section of the State.

In itself, the *Hand Canal* is worthy of note as a great work. It originated in an enlightened perception of the real wants of a declining industry, required engineering skill of a high order, and a vast expenditure of labor and capital for a single company. It is great, too, in the practical results it is now accomplishing. The canal, as completed up to this time (April, 1878,) is about 26 miles in length. The water is taken from Yahoola Creek, at the foot of the Blue Ridge Mountains. It is six feet in width at the water line, and four feet in depth; has a fall of five inches to the 100 feet, and velocity of 30 cubic feet to the second at low water. At Dahlonega it has an elevation of 250 feet above the Yahoola at the same point, and at Findley's Mine, a few miles below, it is 300 feet above the level of the Yahoola, which at this point has so enlarged as to be dignified with the title of river. The reader will form some idea of the power when he contemplates this large body of water foaming along the mountain sides, and ready to be tapped and sent, in a resistless torrent, into the vast depths below. Owing to the rugged nature of the country over which the canal passes, it frequently becomes necessary to conduct this volume of water across immense chasms in order to keep it in its course. This is done by means of large pipes, which are laid down one mountain side, across the valley, and up the opposite elevation until it reaches the desired height, and is discharged into a new section of the canal. There is a pipe near Dahlonega 2,000 feet in length and three feet in diameter. It is made of boiler iron, strong enough to bear the immense pressure. There are also on the line of the canal 7,500 feet of wooden tubing, of a like diameter, and secured by strong wrought-iron bands. Between Dahlonega and the Pigeon Roost mines—the present terminus of the canal—there is another iron tube 2,400 feet in length, and 22 inches in diameter.

The modes of utilizing this water in the operations for gold are various. It is the motive power of the mills where the stamping and washing are done. It serves to carry the ores and gold-bearing earth from the mines to the mills, thus saving the greater part of the cost of transportation. It is also largely used in an operation called "sluicing," where it is turned loose upon the hill-sides, and of its own gravity bears away several feet of the surface earth. For the same purpose a hose and nine-inch pipe is sometimes used, and its power in uprooting trees, bearing down mountains and filling up valleys, is truly wonderful. Often the full force of the canal is turned into a vein containing a day's work of the ore and its rich surroundings, and the whole mass sent roaring down the mountain side into the mill some thousands of feet below. Immense boulders of quartz are sent whirling like so many chips or leaves. This operation not only tears away the earth to the depth of several feet, but at the same time exposes every vein of ore and prepares it for the pick. Every mill is prepared with a receptacle for these washings, from which the water having been drained off, the ores, gravel and sand are shoveled into the troughs and pounded into powder by the immense iron stamps. The pounded contents are then carried by a stream of water over a copper surface upon which there is a coating of quicksilver, with which the fine particles of gold form a mechanical union, and from which they are subsequently liberated by the application of heat, the amalgam having been first scraped from the copper sheets and deposited in a crucible. This is the usual process; there are others, but, as they differ only in details, it is unnecessary to mention them.

The *Hand Canal* is not only used by the mining company who constructed it, but by all the miners on the line, at a moderate rental paid to the proprietors. It is said that in this and other improvements, the Hand Company has invested upwards of a quarter million dollars.

The project of a mint at Atlanta, the seat of government of the State, and on the southern border of the gold belt, is now under discussion in the United States Congress, and should it be established it is estimated that Georgia alone, will furnish a million of gold bullion annually, to aid in keeping it employed.

We might give instances of immense yields of this metal, where parties made fortunes in a day, as it were; but they are exceptional, and calculated to mislead. We prefer to say that the interest is a prosperous one in Georgia when controlled by men of intelligence and a fair share of information in the art of mining.

SILVER has been found on the western slope of the Cohutta mountains, and in Lincoln and some other counties, but not in such quantities as to justify mining.

COPPER.—This metal exists in large quantities in the counties of Fannin, Towns, Cherokee, Paulding, Haralson, Carroll, Greene and Fulton. It is found in combination with iron and sulphur, and in many places constitutes 33 per cent. of the ore, which is often valuable for all three of its component elements. From 5 to 33 per cent. of copper may be considered the extremes. The Fannin county mines are an extension of the celebrated Duck Town veins in the State of Tennessee, and are considered equally rich in that metal.

IRON.—Iron ores, either hematite, limonite, or fossiliferous, are abundant throughout the northern part of the State, and found to a considerable extent in the counties of Harris and Talbot, in Middle Georgia, and in Burke of the Southern division. In the counties of Dade, Walker, and Chattooga, it lies side by side with large deposits of coal, thus affording ample facilities for smelting. In Bartow county we find the best brown hematite, which, in combination with manganese, also abundant in that section, forms that beautiful, mirror-like iron, called by the Germans *Spegelcisen.* The brown hematite is also abundant in Polk county. At the date of the last report, there were in the State 20 iron foundries, with a producing capacity of 300 tons per day, or 100,000 tons of pig-iron per annum, worth, at the market price of $20 per ton, $2,000,000.

COAL.—The discoveries of this mineral have been confined to the three counties of the extreme northwest, to-wit: Dade, Walker, and Chattooga. The supply, though, is so abundant and accessible that it bids fair to be permanent, both for fuel and for mechanical uses. An excellent quality of bituminous coal underlies almost the entire surface of Dade, while in Walker and Chattooga the deposit, though not so abundant, is ample. It is found in largest quantities in Sand Mountain, and in the Lookout range, where two companies, alone, have invested a million of dollars in the business, which is found to be very profitable. One of these mines, belonging to a company of which Ex-Gov. Joseph E. Brown, of Georgia, is President, is worked exclusively by convict labor, at a cost of about 75 cents per day per hand, and yields 300 tons per day. Railroads, with connections leading to all points, have been constructed to the mouths of these mines. A superior article of coke is also prepared on the spot, and shipped to the smelting furnaces of this State and Tennessee. Large quantities of coal from one of these mines have been shipped, within the last two years, to the United States coaling station at Port Royal, in

South Carolina, where it is purchased by the Government for the use of the Navy.

SULPHUR, and Sulphuric Acid, can be obtained in any quantity desired, from the copper and iron ores that contain the former in combination.

GEMS AND PRECIOUS STONES.—Of these, the diamond is found in Hall, White, Lumpkin and Dawson counties; the opal—white, yellow and gray—in Washington county; the beryl in Meriwether; the garnet in Paulding and Cherokee; corundum in Towns, Rabun and Carroll, together with many others of more or less value.

GRAPHITE, of which lead pencils are made, is found in Pickens, Carroll and Elbert counties.

CHROME IRON, for the manufacture of paints, in Habersham and Troup counties.

MISPICKLE, from which arsenic is obtained, in Floyd county.

RUTILE, for coloring artificial teeth, in Lincoln and Habersham counties.

BUHR rock, from which the best mill-stones are cut, exists, in large quantities, in Burke county; also in Stewart, Decatur, and other parts of the Tertiary formation.

ASBESTUS abounds in most of the northern counties, and is being mined in the vicinity of Atlanta, Fulton county. Large quantities are regularly shipped to the Northern States, and there worked up in the manufacture of iron safes, fire-proof paints and roofing, lamp wicks, and, to some extent, into cloth. One of the largest deposits of this mineral, and of the finest quality, is found in Rabun, the extreme northeastern county of the State. It is being mined with much success, the shipments readily commanding $50.00 per ton.

MARBLE.—This mineral exists in exhaustless quantities and of many varieties. It varies in quality from the fine statuary to the coarse-grained used for building. The black marble is found at Tunnel Hill, on the Western & Atlantic Railroad; the red at Dalton; the pink at Varnell's Station, on the East Tennessee & Georgia Railroad, and in Whitfield county. The white, of best quality and in immense supply, near Jasper, Pickens county, on the line of the Marietta & North Georgia Railroad, now in course of construction; also at Buchanan, in Haralson county, and at Van Wert, Polk county.

SERPENTINE, of fine quality and very beautiful, has been recently found in Rabun county.

GRANITE and GNEISS, of the best quality for building, abound in the Northern and Middle divisions of the State, and are convenient to transportation.

SLATE, admirably adapted to roofing, exists in large quantities, and at points accessible. At Rockmart, Polk county, immense shipments are made annually to the various cities and towns of

Georgia and the adjoining States. A railroad connecting with main trunks runs directly to the quarries. On Pine Log Mountain, in Bartow county, about nine miles from the Western & Atlantic Railroad, are other and large deposits, variegated in color, and easily mined. Slate, of good quality, is also found in Gordon county, at points convenient for shipment.

LIMESTONE:—Immense beds exist throughout all the northwestern counties, and there is a fair distribution of it in nearly every section of the State. Large quantities of it are annually burned into lime for building and agricultural purposes, and much of it is equal to the best to be found in the market. At Kingston, Bartow county, Mr. G. H. Warring is largely engaged, in connection with his lime works, in the manufacture of Howard's Hydraulic Cement, an article that has come into extensive use, and has won a deserved popularity.

CALCAREOUS MARLS, or marls composed of shells and other secretions of marine animals, and which receive their value for agricultural purposes from the lime, magnesia, and phosphoric acid, with a certain proportion of soluble silica and organic matter which they contain, are found, in immense beds, in many sections of the State, and in localities where they can be readily utilized for fertilizing purposes. All these deposits exist in the southern half of the State, or below an elevation of 300 feet above the ocean. They are found in Washington, Crawford and Houston, near the centre; in Burke, Scriven and Effingham, in the east; in Charlton, in the southeast; in Clay, Dougherty, Macon and Quitman, in the southwest, and in Muscogee, Chattahoochee and Stewart, in the west. Applied, in combination with a due amount of vegetable matter, these marls are more permanent in their effect upon the lands than any other fertilizer know to the public. The marls of Houston, Stewart, and some other counties in the southwest, contain from six to eight per cent of that valuable fertilizer known as "Green Sand," or the silicate of potash in combination with phosphoric acid. It exists in greatest quantities in the Chattahoochee river deposits.

CLAY.—Kaoline, of the finest quality for the manufacture of porcelain ware, and in the preparation of wall paper, and for other purposes, exists in large and convenient strata in Baldwin and Washington counties, near the centre of the State, and in Cherokee, Pickens and Union, in the north. Another variety of white clay, suitable for the manufacture of fire-brick, furnace-lining and water-pipes, is also found in Washington and Baldwin counties, and a large deposit of the same in Richmond. The gray clay used in making pottery, etc., abounds in Washington, Burke, and in many counties in the south-eastern portion of the state. Red and yellow clays, suitable for building-brick, are found in nearly every county in the State, and in most of them without limit as to quantity.

MEDICINAL WATERS.

In this respect, Nature seems to have provided for the inhabitants of Georgia a mitigation, if not a remedy, for nearly every ill to which human flesh is heir. Our mineral springs are innumerable, and, in variety, correspond with the multifarious ores of the States. In many instances they possess remarkable curative virtues, and are so distributed over the State as to be accessible to all the people. In Butts county (Middle Georgia), convenient to those who dwell in that section of the State which is most exposed to malarial influence (Southern Georgia), we have the Indian Spring, the waters of which are used with great benefit by those who suffer from rheumatic, liver and cutaneous affections; while in the western portion of the same section, in Meriwether county, there is one of the finest warm springs on the continent. It is situated on a spur of Pine Mountain, has a temperature of 90° Fahrenheit, and the supply of water is immense, estimated at 1,400 gallons per minute. There are six splendid baths, ten feet square each, and the waters, which are classed as Carbonated Chalybeate, are highly beneficial in cases of rheumatism, neuralgia, gout, dyspepsia, and diseases of the urinary organs. There are, also, in the same county, a white suphur and a chalybeate spring, both of which are much resorted to.

The entire northern section of the State abounds in mineral waters, a few sulphur, but, for the most part, iron, magnesia, and, in the northwest, limestone. Very many of these springs have been fitted up with elaborate improvements for the accommodation of the public, and thousands resort to them annually in :pursuit of health and amusement. Among the most note may be mentioned Madison Springs, chalybeate, in Madison county; Ponce de Leon Spring, in Fulton county, said to afford great relief in dyspepsia and kidney diseases; New Holland, White Sulphur and Gower Springs, in Hall county; Cohutta Springs, in Murray county; Porter Springs, in Lumpkin county; Catoosa Springs, in Catoosa county—our best improved watering place, with twenty four different varieties of mineral water; Gordon Springs, in Whitfield county, and Rowland Springs, in Bartow county. Nearly all of these watering places are either on, or within a short distance of, some one of our railroads, and can be reached with but little fatigue of travel.

A freestone spring, about a half-mile southeast of Dahlonega, Lumpkin county, registers a temperature of 55° Fahrenheit, which is, probably, the lowest to be found in the State.

WATER POWERS.

In view of what has already been said of the face of the country —the difference in elevation between the mouths and the sources of our rivers ranging from 1,000 to 3,000 feet—it is reasonable to conclude, from such data alone, that the water-powers of Georgia, if equaled, are not excelled by those of any other American State And such is the fact, as will fully appear from the official measure ments of the State Geologist :

"The principal water powers of Georgia are found north of a line passing through Columbus, Macon and Augusta. The waters of the branches, creeks and small rivers of this elevated region are accumulated several hundred feet above the ocean level, and precipitated from the tough metamorphic rocks upon the lower Tertiary country below, thus forming some of our most gigantic water powers, at an elevation entirely free from malaria, and immediately surrounded by the cotton-growing regions of Carolina, Georgia and Alabama.

"The estimates given below are for the theoretical horse power of the stream, without the accumulation of its waters in a reservoir. The horse-power is equivalent to 33,000 foot-pounds.

Chattahoochee river, Columbus... 35,552	horse-power.
Chattahoochee river, Fulton county.......... 2,448	" "
Ocmulgee river, Lloyd's shoals........... 3,970	" "
Ocmulgee river, Seven Islands 2.040	" "
Ocmulgee river, Capp's Shoals................ 508	" "
Ocmulgee river, Glover's mill...... 1,368	" "
Etowah river, Bartow county .. ..·.... 2,250	" "
Etowah river, Franklin mines 1,029	" "
Etowah river, Lumpkin county.. 272	" "
Holt's Shoals, Bibb county................... 1,050	" "
South River, Butts county......... 350	" "
South River, Clarke's Factory................ 247	" "
Snake creek, Carroll county.................. 405	" "
Pataula creek, Clay county................... 601	" "
Armuchee creek, Floyd county............... 151	" "
Coosawattee, Carter's mill................... 3,085	" "
Oconee river, Long Shoals Factory..... 1,024	" "
Oconee river, Riley's shoals................. 2,054	" "
Oconee river, Oconee county................. 5,642	" "
Oconee river, Jackson county................. 271	" "
Tallulah river, Habersham county.. 20,508	" "
Mulberry creek, Harris county................ 1,020	" "
Towaliga, High Falls........................... 1,530	" "
Yellow River, Cedar Shoals..... 1,302	" "
Yellow River, Cedar and Henley shoals....·... 2,000	" "
Little River, Eatonton Factory...... 155	" "
Nacoochee Gold Mining Co., White county.... 575	" "
Savannah river, Augusta canal................14,000	" "

These are only a few of the many which might be mentioned.

The immense water-power of Anthony's Shoals, Broad river, in Wilkes and Elbert counties, has not been accurately estimated.

MANUFACTURES

A purely agricultural country, with slave labor as its main dependence—as Georgia was until a very recent date—is unfavorable to progress in manufactures and the mechanic arts. The cultivation of the soil yields such handsome returns, that the surplus capital of the planter has no motive for seeking other investments. It is, therefore, converted into new lands, which are abundant and cheap, and more negroes to work them; and under the system no people ever attained to independence and wealth more rapidly. Habit, too, is a hard master, and when combined with interest, an absolute one.

Such was our condition as a people previous to the late civil war. That resulted in the freedom of the negro race, and in an entire change in our system of labor, as well as the destruction of our wealth and the desolation of our homes. With the great body of our people, from a variety of causes not necessary to be enumerated in this place, agriculture has not proved profitable under the new system of free black labor. Capital and industry are, therefore, looking to other channels of employment, especially since the production of cotton has attained to, if it has not exceeded, the full measure of the world's demand. Northern capital, too, which accumulated immensely during the war while ours suffered and disappeared, has, of late years, sought new fields; and none have presented greater promise than the utilization of the grand water-powers of Georgia, in the business of manufacturing, especially of our great staple, cotton, and at the very place of its production. This idea obtained some foothold in Georgia many years ago, and gave rise to our earliest essays in the manufacture of cotton. The first factory was built on the Oconee river, four miles below Athens, in the year 1827. This proved successful, and was soon followed by others in the same county (Clark) and in Greene, Richmond, and other counties. From small beginnings these enterprises have developed into considerable magnitude of late years, and with a pecuniary success that points to them as the agents of a new and most prosperous era in the history of our State. The splendid water-powers of the Savannah, at Augusta, and the Chattahoochee, at Columbus, especially, could not long fail to attract the attention of a people alive to their own interests, and to the general welfare.

Georgia has great advantages, in this respect, over the New England States, which have heretofore manufactured most of the American cotton and wool fabrics. We have the cotton at hand, and can buy all we need at the mill, without the cost of transportation and the profits of middle-men. Wages are lower here than in New England. The cost of either water or steam power is less, and also the cost of building materials of every kind. The expense of living is less. The climate is more favorable for the business, and our machinery is never obstructed by ice. In addition to these important advantages, the consumers of our manufactured products are at our very doors. For these reasons, the manufacture of cotton, wool, iron and wood are obliged to constitute important interests in our State, at no distant day.

We have already made greater progress in manufacturing than any other Southern State, as will be seen from the following statistics collected from reliable sources :

There are already organized and in operation in the State, 37 cotton factories; 14 wool factories; 7 paper factories (not including an extensive one in South Carolina owned almost exclusively in Georgia); 28 foundries and manufactories of iron ; 1,400 flour-mills, with over 2,000 run of stones; 734 saw-mills; 34 gold quartz-mills, with 337 stamps. In addition to these, we have railroad, locomotive and car factories and work-shops; plough and cotton-gin factories; carriage and wagon factories; boot and shoe, and sash and blind factories, in large numbers. There are also tanneries, potteries, liquor and turpentine distilleries in great number. In Bartow county there is an extensive factory for the manufacture of hydraulic cement; it is doing a large business, and turning out an article of superior quality. There are also extensive establishments for the manufacture of fertilizers at Savannah, Rome, Bartow county and Augusta.

These are the leading manufacturing interests of Georgia. Although all industries are laboring under depression, to a greater or less extent, at the present time, in any of those named a skilful workman will seldom fail to procure employment, with remunerative wages.

TRANSPORTATION.

There are few things of greater interest to the citizen than the facilities for traveling, and getting the products of his industry to market. No man is willing to live in a country where he can leave home only at a great inconvenience and expense, or where he is compelled to consume a great part of the value of his produce in finding a purchaser.

In this particular, Georgia is peculiarly favored. Her natural and her artificial channels of commerce are rarely surpassed in any country.

RIVER NAVIGATION.

There is a good and safe inland navigation along the Georgia coast, from Savannah to Florida, connecting with the river St. John's, of the latter State, a distance of about 200 miles.

The river Savannah is navigable by steamers the year round from its mouth to Augusta, a distance of about 250 miles, and thence, by flat or "keel" boats, to its confluence with the Broad, about 100 miles further by water.

The Altamaha and its tributary, the Ocmulgee, are navigable by steamers to Hawkinsville, in Pulaski county, a distance of 340 miles, and will soon be open to Macon, some 60 miles higher up. The Oconee, another tributary of the Altamaha, is open to steamers to the Central Railroad bridge, in Washington county, a distance of 340 miles from Darien.

The Chattahoochee, including the Apalachicola, is navigable from the Gulf of Mexico to Columbus, a distance of 400 miles.

Th Flint is navigable 150 miles, to Albany, in Dougherty county, and can be readily opened to a much higher point.

The Coosa runs 40 miles in Georgia, and is open to Greensport, Alabama. Its tributary, the Oostanaula, is navigable 105 miles above Rome, and work is now progressing to open it 30 miles further.

In addition to these, may be mentioned the Satilla, St. Mary's, Ocholochnee, Ohoopee and Ogeechee rivers, aggregating about 150 miles, making a total of about 2,000 miles of river navigation within the State.

RAILROADS.

The State of Georgia is literally covered over with a net-work of railroads. There are but a few portions of it where a loaded wagon cannot reach the cars, discharge, and return home the same day, while to a very large proportion of our people the con-venience of a railroad is carried to their very doors.

Georgia has 2,396 miles of railroad completed and in operation, or about one mile of road to every 488 inhabitants. They pene-trate every section of the State, except certain mountainous coun-ties in the northern division, through which, however, a line has been surveyed, and is nearly graded its entire length, from Ma-rietta, on the Western and Atlantic Railroad, to the town of Mur-phey, in the State of North Carolina. If the roads in operation were uniformly distributed, there would be 18 miles to the county ; the average distance of every farm from a railroad would be six miles, and the greatest distance twelve miles.

RAILROADS IN GEORGIA.

Western & Atlantic, from Atlanta to Chattanooga, Tenn.....138 miles.
Rome Branch, from Kingston to Rome................ ..... 20 "
Cherokee R. R., from Cartersville to Rockmart...... .... 23 "
A. & R. Air-Line, from Atlanta to Charlotte—in Ga........100 "
North-Eastern, from Athens to Lula City .... 40 "
Elberton Air-Line, from Elberton to Toccoa City......... 51 "

Georgia, from Augusta to Atlanta..........................171 miles.
Washington Branch, from Barnett to Washington... .... 18 "
Athens Branch, from Union Point to Athens................ 39 "
Savannah & Augusta, from Augusta to Millen.............. 53 "
Georgia Central, from Savannah to Atlanta..................295 "
Sandersville Branch, from Tennille to Sandersville.......... 3 "
Eatonton Branch, from Gordon to Eatonton................. 39 "
Thomaston Branch, from Barnesville to Thomaston.......... 16 "
Savannah, Griffin and N. Ala., from Griffin to Carrollton..... 60 "
Savannah & Skidaway, from Savannah to Isle of Hope........ 9 "
Montgomery Branch, from Isle of Hope to Montgomery.... 4 "
Atlantic & Gulf, from Savannah to Bainbridge............237 "
Live Oak Branch, from Lawton to Live Oak, Fla............ 48 "
Albany Branch, from Thomasville to Albany................ 60 "
Macon & Augusta, from Macon to Camak, Ga. R. R........ 74 "
Macon & Brunswick, from Macon to Brunswick..............186 "
Hawkinsville Branch, from Cochran to Hawkinsville........ 10 "
Brunswick & Albany, from Brunswick to Albany............172 "
South-Western, from Macon to Eufaula, Ala................140 "
Muscogee Branch, from Fort Valley to Columbus............ 71 "
Perry Branch, from Fort Valley to Perry.................. 11 "
Albany Branch, from Smithville to Albany........ .... 23½ "
Arlington Branch, from Albany to Arlington.... .... 35¾ "
Fort Gaines Branch, from Cuthbert to Fort Gaines.......... 22 "
North & South, from Columbus to Kingston.............. . 20 "
Selma, Rome & Dalton, from Dalton to Selma, Ala.—in Ga., 67 "
Atlanta & West Point, from Atlanta to West Point...... ... 86¾ "
East Tennessee, from Dalton to Bristol, Va.—in Ga.......... 18 "
Chattanooga & Alabama, from Chattanooga to Selma, Ala.—
    in Georgia............... .... 25 "
Dodge's R. R., from Eastman, Dodge Co., to Ocmulgee R.
    (completed).................... .... 10 "

Besides these railroads, in actual operation, there are upwards of
200 miles now under construction, all of which will be finished at
an early day, when Georgia's system of railroad transportation
will be complete. It will be seen that through these agencies the
State is already in direct steam communication with every section
of the Union.

CANALS.

Until recent years, Georgia has given very little attention to
this mode of transportation. Many years ago, a short canal of
sixteen miles was constructed from the Savannah river, at Savannah, to the Ogeechee river, and it is still in use, chiefly for the
transportion of timber and fire-wood, which are floated through
in the form of rafts, or on flat-boats.

About the same time, or at an earlier date, a canal was dug from the Altamaha to Brunswick, but the soil was found too porous to hold water, and after the expenditure of much money the project was abandoned as a failure.

The Augusta canal, completed in 1875, is a great work. It was constructed wholly at the expense of the corporation of Augusta, for the purpose of utilizing the waters of the Savannah, on the banks of which that city is built, for manufactures of the various descriptions, and especially of cotton. It is supplied with water from the Savannah river, is nine miles in length, 150 feet wide at at the top, and 100 wide at the bottom, with 11 feet depth of water, the supply of which is inexhaustible. It has a minimum of 14,000 horse power, and has an available fall of from 13 to 40 feet at various localities along the line. The city leases the water-powers to such works as may be erected on or near its banks, and extensive cotton and flour mills, machine works, and fertilizer manufactories have already been established. This power will, in time, make Augusta one of the leading manufacturing cities of the Union. Through this canal the river boats from above are also admitted to the city, thus avoiding the difficult navigation through the shoals that obstruct the river just above the city.

The project of connecting the waters of the Mississippi with those of the Atlantic ocean, thus avoiding the long and costly land transportation across the Northern States, on the one hand, and the perilous navigation of the Mexican Gulf and West India route, on the other, has long occupied the attention of Southern and Western statesmen and political economists. Georgia approaches nearer to the great western rivers than any other State on the Atlantic coast, and the idea of floating the immense trade of the Mississippi and its tributaries across her territory and through her seaports, is certainly worthy of serious attention.

Of late years, this idea has crystalized into something practical, and there is a good prospect that we shall realize its consummation at no distant day. The interest of the Federal Government is enlisted in the enterprise, and, some two years ago, Congress made an appropriation for the survey of a route for an "Atlantic and Great Western Canal." This survey has been completed by the government engineers, and they have made their report, in which they declare a canal connecting the navigable waters of the Tennessee river (a tributary of the Mississippi) with the head of navigation on the Ocmulgee river (a tributary of the Altamaha which empties into the Atlantic) "eminently practicable," and at a "reasonable cost." Between the Tennessee and the Coosa rivers, the distance is 51 miles, but 17 of which will be actual canal, the rest slack-water. Between the Etowah (a branch of the Coosa) and the Yellow river (a tributary of the Ocmulgee which empties into the Altamaha) there is a distance of 100 miles, only 20 miles of which will be canal, the remaining 80 slack-water. The government engineers are now engaged in removing obstructions from, and deepening, the channels of these several rivers, preparatory to a commencement of work on the canal. This canal, when finished, will be the shortest and cheapest line of water communication between the Atlantic and the Mississippi valley; it will be open to navigation throughout the year, when Northern canals are closed by ice, and Northern trains are obstructed by snows. Through this canal, the exhaustless mines of copper, iron, manganese and coal, of Georgia and Alabama, will be able to compete with the rest of the world, whilst the planters of the West will no longer have reason to complain that the profits of their grain are consumed in the cost of transportation. It is estimated that a bushel of wheat can be profitably carried through this canal, when finished, from the Mississippi to an Atlantic port, for 6½ cents, while it now requires 15 cents to land a bushel in New York. The same difference will obtain in other freights, and the reader may calculate for himself the effect of such a work upon the general prosperity of the South and West.

POPULATION.

The population of Georgia, as stated in the census of 1870—the last taken—numbers 1,184,109. Of these 638,926 are white, and 595,192 black and mulatto. The white population of the coast country are the descendants of original settlers from England, Scotland and the German speaking nations of Europe, with a considerable admixture of families from the Northern States of the American Union. Middle Georgia was settled chiefly by immigrants from Maryland, Virginia and the Carolinas, while in Upper Georgia, whose settlement is of a very recent date, the inhabitants came chiefly from Tennessee and North and South Carolina.

Of the character of the people, it may be said that they are intelligent, industrious, energetic, home-loving, and hospitable. Strangers never fail to receive a hearty welcome in Georgia, nor to make friends, where their conduct is such as to commend them to others. No part of our population appears to feel more at home, and to pursue their various callings with a stronger confidence of success, than the natives of foreign lands who have crossed the great water and cast their lots in this favored land. Their examples of industry, economy, cheerfulness, and respect for law, have made them useful members of society, and large contributors to the energy and wealth of the State. Georgia always receives such accessions to her population with open arms, and readily adopts them as parts of her great repubican famly. In answer ot one of a series of questions recently sent from this Department to intelligent citizens in every county in the State, the almost unanimous response was, that the people desire immigration, and are prepared to extend a hearty welcome to all honest and industrious settlers from other countries.

Georgians are, emphatically, a reading and thinking people, especially in matters involving their own political government. In no State in the Union do the people take a more lively interest in public affairs. Few States have contributed more great men to the national councils, and from the date of Indpendence till now, her soldiers have always ranked among the first on the field of battle. Our people are always equal to the occasion when it calls for brave or virtuous deeds, for acts of duty, or of kindness, or for personal sacrifice for the public good. No people ever turned their backs upon the desolations of war, and began the battle of life anew with stronger arms and stouter hearts than they; and in no other Southern State has such progress been made in the work of recuperation.

The negro population is receiving, equally with the whites, the benefits of the public school fund, are rapidly improving in intelligence, and becoming more efficient as field laborers under wise and just management and close supervision by employers.

HEALTH.

The idea obtains, among those who have not taken the trouble to inform themselves on the subject, that Georgia, because she is a Southern State, has an unwholesome atmosphere, making health insecure within her borders. This objection we have somewhat anticipated in our remarks on climate. There could be no greater error, as a comparison of vital statistics will abundantly show. The health of Georgia will average quite as well as that of any State in the Union. Our citizens of Northern nativity will sustain us in this declaration. The great diversity of climate, resulting from a gradual elevation from the seacoast to the Piedmont country, amounting to from 1,600 to 1,800 feet, precludes the idea of a malarious country. In the low country, immediately along the lines of rivers and swamps, it is conceded that the atmosphere is impure, and that such districts are subject to remittent and intermittent fevers during the summer and fall months; these, however, are generally of a mild type, and readily yield to proper medical treatment. But, owing to the favorable. face of the country in this section of the State, being plentifully supplied with hills and highlands, even those who cultivate the swamps and river bottoms, can fix their residences in the vicinity where they will

3

not be exposed to their malarial influences. And these influences are being rapidly annihilated, year after year, by draining and reducing to dry culture the swamps, which, when thus reclaimed, become both harmless and among the most productive lands in the State. There are large districts that were considered next to uninhabitable thirty years ago from this cause, but which are now filled with a thriving population, who find no difficulty in residing in them the year round.

These latter remarks apply exclusively to the Southern division of the State; in Middle and Upper Georgia, the atmosphere is as pure and wholesome, and the health of the inhabitants as perfect and uninterrupted, as on any portion of the continent. Indeed, these sections, especially the latter, are favorite resorts of invalids and pleasure-seekers during the summer and early fall months, from all parts of the South; while the pine lands of Southern Georgia are annually visited in winter by large numbers from the Northern States suffering from pulmonary affections, rheumatism, etc. Consumption is a disease almost unknown in Georgia, except when imported from other States. In Middle and Northern Georgia are to be found all our medicinal springs and watering places, and thousands annually throng to them in search of health or recreation. Under a theory that has obtained much favor among medical men of late years, that weak or diseased lungs require light and pure, rather than warm, air, the direction of pulmonary invalids has been considerably changed from the semitropical to the Piedmont region, during the winter months. The town of Marietta, in Cobb county, 1,132 feet above the sea, has for years been resorted to by that class of invalids, while the hotel at Mt. Airy, in Habersham county, 1,588 feet above the sea, was well patronised during the past winter by consumptives, and with happy results.

For the information of those who object to Georgia on the score of latitude and its supposed unhealthiness, we would institute a single, but most striking, comparison: The State of Michigan, in the extreme northern portion of the Union, and bordering on Canada, with an atmosphere purified by perpetual breezes from the surrounding lakes, is esteemed to be one of the healthiest States in the Union. Her population and that of Georgia, according to the last census, approximate so nearly that there is a difference of but just *fifty* souls, and the vital statistics of the two States, respectively, show that their death rates are about the same. It is difficult to answer such facts and figures as these, and ignorance and prejudice must give way to truth founded on actual experience.

EDUCATION.

Every man who has a proper regard for the welfare of his posterity, in selecting a home for himself and family, will be influenced, in a large measure, by the facilities which it offers for the education of his children. In this respect, also, Georgia presents peculiar advantages, such as are enjoyed to a very limited extent in newly-settled countries, and superior, in all respects, to those of the other Southern States of the Union. To elaborate her system would require a volume, and we shall only glance at its various features.

The University of Georgia, located at Athens, in Clark county, was incorporated and endowed by a donation of public lands, 40,000 acres, in the year 1784, or soon after the province was organized as a State. It has a permanent endowment of $370,552.17. It has five Educational Departments, thirteen professors, and over two hundred students. The curriculum of studies is thorough. It admits "fifty meritorious young men of limited means," and "young men who design to enter the ministry, of any religious denomination," free of charge for tuition. The college libraries contain about 20,000 volumes.

Connected with the University is the State College of Agriculture and the Mechanic Arts, with its Experimental Farm and Workshops. It has three Departments, viz.: Agriculture, Engineering, and Applied Chemistry, each with a regular course. The tuition in this school is made free to as many young men of the State as there are Representatives (175) and Senators (44) in the Legislature, and the students of both the University proper and the Agricultural and Mechanical Schools have, each, free admission to the instruction given in the other.

There are, also, a Law School, at Athens, and a Medical School, at Augusta, connected with the State University.

The North Georgia Agricultural College, at Dahlonega, Lumpkin county, at which near three hundred students are now being educated free of charge, is also attached to the State University and governed by the same board of trustees. It is proposed to establish a similar school at a point more convenient than either Athens or Dahlonega to pupils residing in the southern half of the State, and it will no doubt be carried into effect at some future day. Military tactics are taught both at Athens and Dahlonega as a part of the regular course, and competent professors are provided in that department.

Mercer University is located at Macon, Bibb county, was established by the Baptist church, and is wholly under the control of that denomination of Christians. It has nine professors, and the course of instruction is thorough. Attached to it are a Law and a Theological Department, at Macon, and Preparatory schools at Penfield, in Greene county, and at Dalton, in Whitfield county. Its libraries, contain about 12,000 volumes; the buildings and grounds cost $150,000; endowment, $160,000. The institution enjoys a large patronage, a considerable portion of which is received from other denominations.

EMORY COLLEGE, at Oxford, Newton county, belongs to the Methodist Episcopal Church, South, and is the joint property of the North Georgia, South Georgia, and Florida Conferences. Like the other colleges of the State, it is well supplied with apparatus, has a good library, and is well patronized.

PIO NONO COLLEGE, at Macon, as its name imports, is a Roman Catholic institution, but recently established. It is well supported by our citizens of that religious faith, and bids fair to rank well among Georgia's institutions of learning.

To the above may be added the *Atlanta University*, established by northern donations for the education of the blacks, male and female, and supported, in part, by appropriations from the State Treasury. Its course of instruction, classical and mathematical, is very thorough. It has 4 professors, 9 teachers, a good library, and the classes of 1877–78 numbered, in the aggregate—

FEMALE COLLEGES.—For the education of females in the higher branches, we have a number of colleges, well distributed over the State. We mention the Wesleyan Female ¡College, at Macon, the first female colllege ever ever established in Georgia; Cherokee Baptist Female College, at Rome; Southern Masonic Female College, at Covington; Rome Female College, at Rome; Dalton Female College, at Dalton; Houston Female Colleges, at Perry; Conyers Female College; Young Female College, at Thomasville; Andrew Female College, at Cuthbert; Monroe Female College, at Forsyth; Gordon Institute, at Barnesville; Gainesville College, at Gainesville; Le Vert Female College, at Talbotton; La Grange Female College and Southern Female College, at La Grange; Furlow Masonic Female College, at Americus, and West Point Female College. Nearly all these institutions are flourishing, and turning out annually, in the aggregate, large numbers of well-educated and well-mannered young women to adorn and elevate society.

Besides these, there are large numbers of high schools, both male and female, very many of them ranking among the best institutions of learning in the South.

Nor is Georgia unmindful of her unfortunate children whom nature has stinted in the bestowment of her gifts; nor has she been niggardly in providing for their wants in this respect, and in making them useful to themselves and to others. Large and costly edifices have been erected by the State for the care and education of the blind, and of the deaf and dumb—for the former at Macon, and for the latter at Cave Spring, in Floyd county. Both these unfortunate classes are taught not only in the learning of the schools, but also those useful occupations which render them measurably independent.

There are, also, a goodly number of orphans' homes and schools in the State, maintained by private or denominational benevolence.

PUBLIC SCHOOL SYSTEM.—The Common Schools of Georgia form, by far the most interesting feature of her educational system. Recognizing the great moral and political truth that intelligence and virtue form the basis of all good government, the people of Georgia have inserted in their Constitution, or fundamental law, a provision declaring that "there shall be a thorough system of common schools for the education of children," which "shall be free to all the children of the State," the expenses of which "shall be provided for by taxation, or otherwise." In accordance with this constitutional provision, the necessary laws have been passed, and the system referred to is now in successful and beneficent operation, the whites and the blacks being educated in separate schools. The State appropriates annually, for the support of these free schools, about $300,000, and this sum is supplemented each year by local city and county appropriations to the amount of between $140,000 and $150,000. The number of pupils in actual attendance on these schools last year (1877), was in round numbers, 191,000, of whom 127,000 were whites and 64,000 blacks. The progressive interest in, and usefulness of, the system are illustrated by the statistics of attendance from year to year. In 1871, but seven years ago, when it was put in operation, the number of children taught was but 49,578—42,914 whites and 6,664 blacks. In 1874 the number had increased to 145,541, in 1876, to 179,405; and in 1877, to upwards of 191,000.

The Common School organization extends to every county in the State, and includes every district or subdivision of the counties where the population is sufficiently numerous to admit of a school; so that there is scarcely a child in Georgia who is not within reach of a school where a good education can be obtained free of expense.

In fine, it may be said with truth that, as respects educational facilities and their adaptation to the public wants, the State of Georgia is in advance of all her sister Southern States; while, in this respect, she is progressing year after year, and will soon stand side by side with the older and more favored commonwealths of the North.

RELIGIOŇ.

The laws of Georgia guarantee to the citizen perfect freedom of religious opinion and worship, and there is no political or civil disqualification on account of religious belief. Every denomination is not only tolerated, but protected, in the free enjoyment of faith and worship, As a necessary consequence, there is a complete separation of Church and State, both by law and practically. Each moves in its appropriate sphere, and neither is allowed to encroach on the other.

The principal religious denominations in the State, with their respective numbers, etc., are as follows:

BAPTIST CHURCH.—This is the most numerous religious denomination in the State. It has 114 Associations, 762 ordained ministers, and 279 licentiates, 2,532 churches, 209,790 members—of whom 97,463 are blacks—1 university, 3 high schools, 368 Sunday-schools with 3,695 teachers and 18,674 scholars. (Six Associations not reported.)

METHODIST EPISCOPAL CHURCH, SOUTH.—This church has two Conferences—North Georgia and South Georgia—which, in the aggregate, have 314 traveling preachers, 636 local preachers, 88,148 members, 907 Sunday-schools, 5,631 officers and teachers, 43,106 Sunday-school scholars, 1,033 churches with 279,853 sittings, and church property valued $941,570. It has 1 male college, 5 female colleges, several high schools for both sexes, and two orphan free schools.

The negro members of this denomination, since emancipation, have been formed into an independent organization, under the auspices of the Methodist Episcopal Church South, known as the COLORED METHODIST EPISCOPAL CHURCH OF AMERICA, and number about 14,000.

METHODIST EPISCOPAL CHURCH (North).--This Church has been organized in Georgia since the war. It has 193 church buildings, worth $119,000, 395 preachers, 200 Sunday-schools with 716 officers and teachers and 8,800 scholars. The members number about 15,000, 12,000 of whom are colored. It has one university and five or six schools for colored, and one high school for white pupils.

PROTESTANT METHODIST CHURCH, has a membership of 2,500 persons.

AFRICAN METHODIST EPISCOPAL CHURCH, has 41,000 members and about 100 colored ministers.

PRESBYTERIAN CHURCH.—This Church has 5 presbyteries, 157 church organizations, 149 church edifices with 56,000 sittings, 75 ministers, 5 licentiates, 8,258 members, 88 Sabbath-schools with 4,669 scholars, and church property to the amount of $653,500; annual contributions, $78,643.

THE ASSOCIATE REFORMED PRESBYTERIANS, have 6 churches with 2,000 sittings, 530 members, 5 ministers, and 6 Sunday-schools with 300 scholars.

The colored people of the State have organized a separate presbytery, styled the Knox Presbytery, which has 6 churches, 6 ministers, and about 1,000 members.

THE PROTESTANT EPISCOPAL CHURCH, whose first bishop was elected in 1840, has 31 churches and stations, 33 clergymen, 4,305 communicants, 25 Sunday-schools with 349 teachers and 2,510 scholars; annual contributions, $70,425.34.

THE CHRISTIAN CHURCH has 50 houses of worship, 40 ministers and 5,000 members.

THE ROMAN CATHOLIC CHURCH.—The Diocese of Georgia was organized and the first Bishop appointed in 1850. The rapid progress of the Church is evidenced by its statistics: It has now two splendid cathedrals—in Savannah and Atlanta—23 churches, 35 chapels, 24 priests and 27,500 members. It owns 1 college, 3 male and 7 female schools, 1 orphan asylum, and church property to the amount of $600,000.

THE LUTHERAN CHURCH has 11 church organizations, 10 church edifices, and church property valued at $57,100. We have been unable to ascertain the number of members.

THE CONGREGATIONALISTS have 10 churches with 2,800 sittings, and church property of the value of $16,550.

THE UNIVERSALISTS have 5 church organizations, 3 church edifices with 900 sittings; church property valued at $900.

THE UNITARIANS are few in number, and two churches are all of which we have been able to obtain information. One is located at Augusta, has a fine church edifice for public worship, and a large and wealthy congregation; the other is in Douglas county, but we have no information of its membership or condition.

THE ISRAELITES.—From the best information obtainable, the Jews in Georgia number about 4,500. They have 6 synagogues—2 in Savannah, and 1 each, in Augusta, Atlanta, Macon and Columbus, some of them fine and costly edifices. There are also congregations without synagogues or ministers in a number of the smaller towns, who are supplied, from time to time, by ministers from the five cities named above. Each congregation has its own benevolent society for the aid of the needy and distressed. They have Sabbath-schools of their own, but for secular education, for the most part, patronize the public and private schools of the State.

STATE CHARITABLE INSTITUTIONS.

THE GEORGIA ACADEMY FOR THE BLIND is located at Macon, Bibb county, and is supported almost entirely by the State. Pupils of both sexes, between the ages of 7 and 25 years, are admitted, though males over 25 are received for instruction in the various trades. The pupils are taught all the elementary branches of an English education, together with the Holy Scriptures, history and music. They are also instructed in such mechanical trades as can be imparted to the sightless. The blind are thus redeemed from ignorance through this public charity, and taught to be useful, and even self-supporting. The number of pupils ranges from 60 to 75; number in 1877—62. The school is conducted by a Principal, 2 Professors, 3, assistants, and a Master of Workshops.

DEAF AND DUMB INSTITUTE.—This school is located at Cave Spring, in Floyd county, one of the most romantic and delightful sections of the State. It is also supported by the State, and annually turns out quite a number of this truly unfortunate class, educated sufficiently to enable them to enjoy free intercourse with others, and with occupations by which, with proper industry, they have no difficulty in earning a support. The number of pupils now in attendance is 70. The most approved system of instruction is adopted in this institution, as well as in the Academy for the Blind. Besides the Principal, there are four male teachers, one female teacher and a matron.

LUNATIC ASYLUM.—The State of Georgia, many years ago, erected, at a heavy cost, near Milledgeville, then the seat of government, an Asylum for the care of lunatics, and by means of liberal appropriations, has enlarged the charity from year to year until the inmates have come to number 845, of whom there are whites 710—376 male, and 334 female. The blacks are separately provided for, and number 135, of whom 69 are males, and 66 females. The Asylum is both a home and a hospital. Under skillful physicians and nurses, the patients receive the best of attention, and large numbers are annually restored to health of mind and body. About ten years ago, the Legislature passed an act setting aside the Okefinokee Swamp, containing about 500,000 acres of land—decided to be reclaimable at a small cost compared with its value for timber and agricultural purposes—as a permanent endowment for a State Orphans' Home; owing however, to the fall in the price of lands and general depression of the agricultural interest, the humane intention of the Legislature has never been carried into effect.

BENEVOLENT SOCIETIES.

Associations for mutual aid in times of sickness and distress are numerous in Georgia, and to be found in nearly all the counties of the State. The principal organizations are secret, and as follows:

The FREE AND ACCEPTED MASONS, the most ancient of orders and by far the most numerous in the State, has over 280 lodges and about 15,500 members. There are also eight chartered Commanderies, with 320 members.

THE INDEPENDENT ORDER OF ODD FELLOWS has 48 lodges, and about 2,000 members.

THE KNIGHTS OF PYTHIAS, KNIGHTS OF HONOR and SONS OF MALTA have each lodges in all of the cities and some of the smaller towns of the State, but we have failed to obtain definite information regarding them.

THE INDEPENDENT ORDER OF GOOD TEMPLARS, a benevolent order, with a pledge of total abstinence from intoxicating drinks, has 300 working lodges and a membership numbering 10,000.

Besides these, nearly all the churches have relief societies, and benevolent associations exist in all the cities of the State. A meritorious claim to charity, or temporary aid, is seldom disregarded in Georgia.

GOVERNMENT OF GEORGIA.

The government of Georgia, in common with that of all the States of the American Union, is a Representative Democracy. All officers are chosen directly by the people, or by persons to whom the people, from motives of public policy or convenience, have delegated the power of election.

QUALIFICATION OF VOTERS.—The Constitution of Georgia provides that every male citizen of the United States (except idiots, lunatics, and persons convicted, in any court of competent jurisdiction, of treason against the State, embezzlement of public funds, malfeasance in office, bribery, larceny, or of any crime punishable by imprisonment in the Penitentiary), who is twenty-one years of age, who shall have resided in this State one year next preceding the election, and six months in the county in which he offers to vote, and who shall have paid all taxes that have been legally required of him, and which he has had an opportunity of paying, except for the year of the election, shall be deemed an elector, or person qualified to vote at all general elections.

THE LEGISLATURE.—The Legislative, or law-making power of the State, is vested in a General Assembly, consisting of two houses, a Senate and a House of Representatives, the members of each being chosen once in every two years, on the first Wednesday in October, by the qualified voters of the State. Its sessions are held biennially, commencing on the first Wednesday in November, and cannot be extended beyond the period of forty days, except by a vote of two-thirds of both houses.

The Senators are 44 in number, and chosen from districts composed of contiguous counties for that purpose.

The Representatives are 175 in number, and apportioned among the counties as follows: The six counties having the largest population are entitled to three members each; the twenty-six counties having the next largest population, to two members each; and the remaining one hundred and five counties to one Representative each.

Neither the Senators nor Representatives can be increased in number. Senators must be twenty-five years of age, and four years citizens of this State. Representatives must be twenty-one years of age and two years residents of this State.

THE EXECUTIVE.—The chief Executive power of the State is vested in a Governor, who is elected for two years by the qualified voters of the State, and is ineligible after the expiration of a second term, for the period of four years. He must have been a citizen of the United States fifteen years, of the State six years, and attained the age of thirty years. He has the revision of all bills and resolutions passed by the General Assembly before they become laws, and a two-thirds vote of each house is necessary to override his negative. He has power to grant pardons and reprieves, to commute penalties, remit any part of a sentence, and to remove disabilities imposed by law; in every case his action, and the reasons therefor, to be reported to the General Assembly. The appointing power of the Governor is confined to his own Secretaries and Clerks, the Commissioner of Education, Commissioner of Agriculture, State Geologist, State Librarian, Principal Keeper of the Penitentiary, Judge and Solicitor of the City Court of Atlanta, Judges and Solicitors of the County Courts, Commissioners for McIntosh county and city of Darien, Mayor and Aldermen of St. Mary's, Trustees of the Lunatic Asylum, Trustees of the Academy for the Deaf and Dumb, and Visitors to the State University, Atlanta University, and to the Academies for the Blind and for the Deaf and Dumb. He has also power to fill all vacancies that may occur in other offices during the recess of the Legislature, or until a new election can be held.

The Secretary of State, Comptroller General, Treasurer, and Attorney General are elected by the people, at the same time, in the same manner, and for the same term, with the Governor.

JUDICIARY.—The judicial power of the State is vested in a Supreme Court for the correction of errors in the courts below, in Superior Courts, Courts of Ordinary, Justices' Courts and in Notaries Public, who are ex-officio Justices of the Peace; in some counties in County Courts, and in some cities in City Courts.

The Supreme Court consists of a Chief Justice and two Associate Justices, who are chosen by the General Assembly and hold their offices for six years. There are two sessions of this court each year, held at the Capital.

There are twenty Superior Court Circuits, in each of which there are a Judge and a State Solicitor, elected by the General Assembly every four years. The Superior Court meets in each county, not less than twice in each and every year. It has exclusive jurisdiction in cases of divorce, in criminal cases where the offender is subject to death or imprisonment in the penitentiary, in cases involving the title to lands, and in equity cases. It tries appeals from inferior courts, and has concurrent jurisdiction with them in cases of debt, etc. It may issue writs of *habeas corpus*, *mandamus*, injunction, *scire facias*, and all other writs necessary for carrying its powers into full effect.

An Ordinary is elected by the people of each county, and holds his office for four years. His jurisdiction embraces the probate of wills and the management of estates by executors, administrators and guardians. He has power over roads, bridges, ferries, public buildings, paupers, county funds, county taxes, etc., etc.

The County Court Judges and Solicitors are appointed by the Governor, and the jurisdiction of the former, in civil cases, extends to contracts where the amount claimed as principal does not exceed $200, and to torts where the damage alleged does not exceed $100; to the eviction of intruders and tenants holding over, partition of personalty, the issuing of possessory and distress warrants, attachments of personalty, garnishments, the foreclosure of mortgages on personalty, etc. His criminal jurisdiction embraces that of Justices of the Peace, and, in addition, the trial of offenses below the grade of felony. There are, at present, but two city courts in the State, viz: of Savannah and of Atlanta. The Judge and Solicitor of the City Court of Savannah are elected every three years by the Mayor and Aldermen of the city. The Judge and Solicitor of the City Court of Atlanta are appointed by the Governor, and hold their offices for four years. The jurisdiction of these courts is variously limited by the several acts creating them. The civil jurisdiction in Savannah is limited to cases where the amount involved is $1,000 or under, and is confined to the city; whilst the criminal jurisdiction embraces the county of Chatham, and extends to all crimes not punishable by imprisonment in the Penitentiary. In Atlanta both the civil and the criminal jurisdiction of the court is concurrent with that of the Superior Court, except in cases where the Constitution vests exclusive powers in the latter; and embraces the county of Fulton.

Justices of the Peace are elected by the people, one for each militia district in the State, and hold their offices for four years. Their courts sit monthly, and have jurisdiction in all cases arising under contracts, and in cases of injury to personal property, where the principal sum does not exceed one hundred dollars. They have power to administer oaths, take affidavits, and issue attachments. In criminal matters they are the conservators of the peace in their respective districts and counties, may issue warrants for the arrest of persons charged with crime, examine such persons when brought before them, and commit, bind over, or discharge, according to the law and the evidence.

Notaries Public, one for each militia district, are appointed by the Judges of the Superior Courts upon the recommendation of the grand juries of the respective counties. They hold office for four years, and their jurisdiction and powers are the same with those of Justices of the Peace.

All county officers are elected by the people, and (except the Ordinary) hold their offices for two years. A county officer must be a qualified voter, and must have been a resident of the county for two years next preceding his election.

HOMESTEAD EXEMPTION.

The Constitution of Georgia exempts from levy and sale, by virtue of any legal process whatever, (except in the cases named below,) of the property of every head of a family, or guardian, or trustee of a family of minor children, or every aged or infirm person, or person having the care and support of dependent females of any age, real or personal estate, or both, to the value, in the aggregate, of *sixteen hundred dollars*. Said property, however, is liable to levy and sale for taxes, for the purchase money of the same, for labor done thereon, for material furnished therefor, or for the removal of incumbrances thereon. The exemption includes not only the property itself, but all improvements made thereon after it is set aside. A mortgage of property by the father during his lifetime, cannot, after his death, deprive his minor childred of a homestead, or exemption right in the moitgaged premises.

LEGAL PROVISIONS OF GENERAL INTEREST.

No person shall be deprived of life, liberty, or property, except by due process of law.

Every person has the right to prosecute, or defend, his own cause in any of the courts, in person, by attorney, or both.

Every person charged with an offense against the laws of this State, shall have the privilege and benfit of counsel ; shall be furnished, on demand, with a copy of the accusation, and a list of the witnesses on whose testimony the charge is founded ; shall have compulsory process to obtain the testimony of his own witnesses ; shall be confronted by the witnesses testifying against him, and shall have a public and speedy trial by an impartial jury.

Perfect freedom to worship God according to the dictates of his own conscience, is guaranteed to every citizen.

No inhabitant of this State shall be molested in person, or property, or prohibited from holding any public office or trust, on account of his religious belief.

No law shall ever be passed to curtail, or restrain, the liberty of speech or of the press.

The right of the people to be secure in their persons, houses, papers and effects against unreasonable searches and seizures, shall not be violated; and no warrant shall issue except upon probable cause, supported by oath, or affirmation, particularly describing the place, or places, to be searched, and the person or things to be seized.

The social status of the citizen shall never be the subject of legislation.

There shall be no imprisonment for debt.

The right of the people peaceably to assemble, and, by petition, or remonstrance, apply to the government for a redress of their grievances, shall not be denied.

All citizens of the United States resident in this State are to be considered citizens of this State, and the Legislature shall make all necessary laws for their protection as such.

No conviction shall work corruption of blood or forfeiture of estate.

Private property shall not be taken, nor damaged, for public purposes without just and adequate compensation to the owner.

No *ex post facto* law, or law impairing the obligation of contracts, shall be passed.

No total divorce shall be granted, except on the concurrent verdicts of two juries, at different terms of the court.

Cases respecting titles to land shall be tried in the county where the land lies. All other civil cases shall be tried in the county where the defendant resides, and all criminal cases in the county where the crime was committed, except cases in the Superior court, where the Judge is satisfied that an impartial jury cannot be obtained in the county.

Grand jurors are drawn from the body of the people, and must be experienced, intelligent and upright men. Traverse jurors are drawn in the same way, and must be intelligent and upright men.

Taxes can be imposed for the following purpoess only: For the support of the State government and public institutions; for educational purposes; to pay the interest and the principal of the public debt; to suppress insurrection, repel invasion, defend the State in time of war, and to supply soldiers who lost a limb or limbs in the military service of the Confederate States with substantial artificial limbs during life. Taxes must be uniform on the same class of subjects, and *ad valorem* on all property taxed. A poll tax shall be levied for educational purposes only, and shall never exceed one dollar *per annum*.

The rate of taxation in Georgia, for State purposes, varies from year to year, according to the wants of the government, from 70 cents to 100 cents on each $100 worth of property. The several counties are authorized, in addition, to levy a tax for county purposes, not to exceed fifty per cent. on the amount of State tax levied for the same year.

The State shall contract no debt, except to supply casual deficiences (not to exceed $200,000), to repel invasion, suppress insurrection, and defend the State in time of war, or to pay the existing public debt.

The credit of the State shall not be loaned, or pledged, to any individual, company, corporation, or association; nor shall the State become a joint owner, or stockholder, in any company, association, or corporation.

No county, municipal corporation, or political division, shall incur a debt to exceed seven per cent. of the assessed value of the taxable property therein; and loans by the same to supply casual deficiencies, shall not exceed five per centum.

Any county, municipal corporation, or political division, which shall incur any bonded indebtedness under the Constitution, shall, at or before the time of so doing, provide for the assessment and collection of an annual tax, sufficient in amount to pay the principal and interest of said debt within thirty years from the date of the incurring of said indebtedness.

The General Assembly shall not, by vote, resolution, or order, grant any donation or gratuity in favor of any person, corporation, or association.

A wife, notwithstanding marriage, continues to be the legal owner of the property she possessed at the time of marriage, and of any that may accrue to her by gift, bequest, or her own acquisition, after marriage.

The law creates a lien upon property for taxes, for judgments or decrees of courts, and in favor of laborers, landlords, mortgagees, mechanics, contractors, inn-keepers, merchants and factors for furnishing supplies, and in some other cases.

Titles to land can be passed only by will or deed in writing duly executed. The entailment of estates is prohibited by law. Gifts or grants in tail convey an absolute title.

In making his will, a testator may do what he chooses with his property, except that he cannot prejudice his creditors; and the law considers his wife so far a creditor that he cannot deprive her of dower, except with her consent.

Where a party dies intestate, the law requires his estate to be distributed as follows: After payment of expenses of administration, of a year's support to the family, and the debts of the intestate, the remaining property goes: 1. To the husband or husband's children, if any, of a deceased wife;' 2, to the wife or wife's children of a deceased husband, if any, the wife having one-fifth part of the estate if there be more than four children ; 3, to the children ; 4, to the father, mother, brothers and sisters of the deceased. Children or grand-children represent a deceased distributee, the rule not extending, however, beyond the grand-children of a brother or sister.

Upon the death of an intestate, his widow may elect to take a dower, or one-third interest for life, in the lands of her deceased husband, and share and share alike with the children in the personal property ; or, she may relinquish her right of dower, and take a child's part, share and share alike, in all the property, to be her own absolutely.

Females are not allowed the elective franchise, nor can they hold any civil office, or perform any civil function, unless specially authorized by law ; nor can any military, jury, police, patrol or road duty be required of them.

The legal period of full age is 21 years. Persons between 21 and 45 years of age are liable to military duty ; and between 16 and 50 years, to road duty ; though the law makes certain exemptions from both services.

LAWS OF FORCE IN GEORGIA.

The laws of force in Georgia are thus graduated with reference to their obligation :

1. The Constitution of the United States, the laws of the United States made in pursuance thereof, and all treaties made under the authorities of the United States, comprise the supreme law of the State.

2. The Constitution of this State.

3. Acts and resolutions of the General Assembly of the State, including the Code, and the decisions of the Common Law and and Equity Courts of England prior to May 14th, 1776, when conclusive as to the Common Law, except when changed or modified by statute of the State.

RIGHTS AND EXEMPTIONS OF ALIENS UNDER THE
LAWS OF GEORGIA.

While aliens are denied the right to vote, and hold office, by the laws of Georgia, all other provisions with regard to them are most liberal. So long as their governments are at peace with the United States, and with this State, they are entitled to all the rights of citizens of other States resident in this State. With certain conditions, they can purchase, hold, and convey real estate; they are protected in all their rights of person and of property; they can sue and give evidence in our courts so long as the same comity is extended to our citizens by their governments. They may receive and enforce leins, by mortgage or otherwise, on real estate. They are exempt from military duty, except in the suppression of insurrections and repelling local invasion, and also from service in the courts as grand or traverse jurors.

The conditions on which an alien or unnaturalized person may hold land in this State are thus set forth in our statute:

"An alien may be may be permitted to acquire title to, and hold, lands within this State, upon taking an oath in writing, to be filed in the Clerk's office of the Superior Court of the county in which the land lies, that it is his intention *bona fide* to improve the same; and if said alien shall fail, or neglect, within one year after the purchase aforesaid, to begin such improvement, said land shall become subject to an annual tax of fifty cents per acre for each and every acre so held by him; and, on failure to pay the same, it shall be the duty of the tax collector of said county to set up and expose to sale so much of said land as may be necessary to pay such tax, having first given sixty days notice of the time and place of sale, in one or more of the public gazettes of this State; the overplus, if any there be, after the payment of the tax aforesaid, and the costs accruing thereon, to be deposited with the Ordinary of said county, to be applied to educational purposes, if not called for by the owner thereof within two years after such sale: *Provided*, that no alien shall hold or purchase more than one hundred and sixty acres of land until he had declared on oath his intention to become a citizen."

NATURALIZATION.

The acts of Congress provide that an alien may become a citizen of the United States on the following conditions:

1. He shall declare on oath, before a Circuit or District Court of the United States, or a District or Supreme Court of the Territories, or a court of record in any of the States having common law jurisdiction and a seal and clerk, two years, at least, prior to his admission, that it is *bona fide* his intention to become a citizen of the United States, and to renounce forever all allegiance and fidelity to any foreign prince, potentate, state, or sovereignty, and, particularly, by name, to the prince, potentate, state or sovereignty of which the alien may be at the time a citizen or subject.

2. At the time of making this application, he must take an oath before the same court to support the Constitution of the United

States, and that he entirely renounces and abjures all allegiance and fidelity to any foreign prince, potentate, etc.

3. At the time of admission, he must prove, to the satisfaction of the court, by testimony other than his own, that he has resided in the United States five years at least; that during that time he has maintained a good moral character, and that he is attached to the principles of the Constitution of the United States, and well disposed to the good order and preservation of the same. He must also renounce any hereditary title, or order of nobility, that he may have borne, if any, previous to his admission to citizenship.

4. If the alien be under twenty-one years of age, and has resided in the United States three years previous to his arrival at that age, if he subsequently apply for admission, the three years of his minority will be counted in estimating his five years of residence, and he will be allowed to make the foregoing declarations and oath at the time of his admission.

5. The minor children, or those under twenty-one years of age, of persons who have been duly naturalized, if dwelling in the United States, are held and considered as citizens thereof.

6. By special act of Congress, passed July 17, 1862, any alien of the age of twenty-one years, and upwards, who has enlisted, or may enlist, in the armies of the United States, either the regular or the volunteer forces, and has been, or may be hereafter, honorably discharged, shall be admitted to citizenship upon his petition, without any previous declaration of his intention, and upon proof of only one year's residence in the United States previous to his application to become a citizen, of his good moral character, and that such person has been honorably discharged from the service of the United States.

7. Seamen who have served three years on any merchant vessel of the United States, after making a declaration of their intention, shall be entitled to become citizens upon application, and the production of a certificate of discharge and good conduct during that time, together with a certificate of their declaration of intention to become citizens.

STATE AGRICULTURAL ORGANIZATIONS.

There are two State Agricultural Organizations, viz.: the State Agricultural Society and the State Grange.

The former was organized in 1846, and with the exception of seven years during and after the late war, has continued its active and efficient work to the present time. It is now a representative body, composed of delegates elected annually by local organizations which exist in nearly every county in the State.

It holds semi-annual conventions, one in February, at some

4

point in the lower half of the State, and one in August, in the upper half.

It has accomplished great good to the agricultural interests of the State by these semi-annual conventions, and by its Annual Fairs. The transactions of this society, all of which have been published since 1872, constitute a valuable contribution to Southern agricultural literature.

THE STATE GRANGE.

This is a secret Agricultural Organization, known as the Patrons of Husbandry, composed of representatives, ladies and gentlemen, from local granges.

Its general objects are the same as those of the State Society, but attendance upon its meetings is confined to members of the order of Patrons of Husbandry, while those of the Society are open to the public. This organization, too, has rendered valuable service to the agriculturists by securing concert of action and more general co-operation among the farmers of the State. It is, however, less active at this time than it was a few years after its organization.

NORTH GEORGIA STOCK AND FAIR ASSOCIATION.

This is a joint stock Association recently organized with $40,000 stock. This is, financially, a very strong organization, the leading object of which is the improvement of the live stock of the State.

DISTRICT AND COUNTY ORGANIZATIONS.

Besides the county Societies, neighborhood clubs and Granges, some of which are to be found in nearly every county in the State, there are, especially in Middle and Southwestern Georgia, many district and county Fair Associations, which are doing much to stimulate progressive agriculture and horticulture.

THE GEORGIA STATE HORTICULTURAL SOCIETY.

This society was chartered and organized as a joint stock association in 1876.

It is devoted to the encouragement of profitable vegetable and fruit production in the State, and, though now only about to complete the second year of its existence, it has, by the concerted labors of the most advanced and intelligent horticulturists of the State, materially stimulated systematic fruit culture, which had previously been so sadly neglected. Partly as the result of the work of this society, the planting of fruit trees during the last winter and spring far exceeded that of any previous season in the history of the state.

DEPARTMENT OF AGRICULTURE.

As the result of the persistent recommendations of the State Agricultural Society and the State Grange, the Governor of the State recommended in his annual message and the Legislature established by law, a Department of Agriculture in 1874, the first of its kind established in any State in the Union. It is presided over by a Commissioner whose duties are elaborately defined by law.

This Department now about to complete its fourth year has, by its work, in promoting advanced agriculture, become firmly fixed in the hearts of the people, who, somewhat indifferent towards it when first established, now regard it as one of the most important and useful branches of the State government.

The Commissioner has the general supervision of the inspection and analysis of fertilizers and has, by systematic and vigilant execution of the laws relating to the same, not only afforded ample protection to the farmers against the sale of spurious or fraudulent commercial fertilizers, but has caused to be paid into the treasury of the State more than $22,000 after deducting the expenses of inspection and analysis and the annual appropriation of $13,200 to the Department, the total income from that source during the season just ended being about $45,000.

The publications issued from the Department and distributed among the farmers of the State have been of an instructive character, and have been highly appreciated not only by the people of Georgia, but have been eagerly sought by those of other States. The "Manual of Sheep Husbandry in Georgia" has given an impetus to that industry never before known in the State, and is attracting capital from other States for investment in the cheap lands and perennial pastures so well adapted to this important industry. The "Manual on the Hog", and other pamphlets issued by the Commissioner, have attracted much attention, both in Georgia and elsewhere. Those containing the analyses of fertilizers, formulæ for composts and the results of the soil tests of fertilizers, have been especially sought by the farmers of Georgia and other Southern States.

A "Hand Book of Georgia" was issued by the Commissioner in 1876, in which is given a full account of the varied resources of the State, its condition and institutions. This book supplies a want long felt by the people of Georgia, and furnishes reliable information to those in search of the most propitious field of immigration. The demand for this work has been so great that the first and second editions were speedily exhausted, and yet the demand continues.

These various publications have attracted the attention of the reading public in the Northern States of the Union and many, who were looking to the West as the most inviting field for emigrants, are now making inquiry in regard to Georgia preparatory to seeking homes among us.

GEOLOGICAL SURVEY.

The office of State Geologist was created in 1874, a Geologist appointed, and the active work of making a "careful and complete geological, mineralogical and physical survey of the State" begun.

Some of the results of this survey have already been given in this work in the chapter on mineral resources, water powers, woods, etc.

Its investigations have developed wealth before neither known nor appreciated by the people of the State, and, though but little more than half completed, it is impossible to estimate the benefits that have accrued to the State and its people.

The effects of the labors of the State Geologist during the last four years will be felt by future generations. Capital, in large amounts, has already sought investment in our rich mining lands, and our water powers will attract still more.

The survey has developed the fact that Georgia is not only rich in agricultural resources, but unsurpassed in mineral wealth and manufacturing facilities.

NEWSPAPERS—1878.

The following list comprises all the newspapers printed in Georgia at the present time, with their places of publication alphabetically arranged. It will be seen that there are 9 dailies, 2 tri-weeklies, and 114 weeklies—total, 125. Most of the dailies publish tri-weeklies, and both dailies and tri-weeklies have weekly editions :

Alapaha (Berrien county)—*News*, weekly.

Albany—*News*, weekly ; *Advertiser*, weekly.

Americus—*Sumter Republican*, tri-weekly and weekly.

Athens—*Southern Banner*, weekly ; *Chronicle*, weekly ; *Watchman*, weekly.

Atlanta—*Constitution*, daily ; *Independent*, weekly ; *Republican*, weekly ; *Sunny South*, weekly ; *Christian Index*, weekly : *Methodist Advocate*, weekly ; *Planter and Grange*, weekly; *Southern Enterprise*, monthly ; *Homeward Star*, monthly.

Augusta—*Chronicle and Constitutionalist*, daily ; *Evening News*, daily.

Bainbridge—*Democrat*, weekly.

Barnesville—*Gazette*, weekly.

Blakely—*Early County News*, weekly.

Brunswick—*Appeal*, weekly.
Buena Vista—*Argus*, weekly.
Butler—*Herald*, weekly.
Calhoun—*Times*, weekly.
Canton—*Cherokee Georgian*, weekly.
Carnesville—*Franklin County News*, weekly.
Carrollton—*Times*, weekly.
Cartersville—*Express*, weekly ; *Free Press*, weekly.
Cave Spring—*Enterprise*, weekly.
Cedar Town—*Record*, weekly ; *Express*, weekly.
Columbus—*Enquirer-Sun*, daily ; *Times*, daily.
Conyers—*Examiner*, weekly ; *Weekly*, weekly.
Covington—*Star*, weekly ; *Enterprise*, weekly.
Crawfordville—*Democrat*, weekly.
Cumming—*Georgia Methodist*, weekly.
Cuthbert—*Appeal*, weekly ; *True Southron*, weekly.
Dahlonega—*Signal*, weekly.
Dalton—*Enterprise*, weekly ; *North Georgia Citizen*, weekly.
Darien—*Timber Gazette*, weekly.
Dawson—*Journal*, weekly.
Douglasville—*Medium*, weekly.
Dublin—*Post*, weekly ; *Gazette*, weekly.
Eastman—*Times*, weekly.
Eatonton—*Broad-Axe and Itemizer*, weekly.
Elberton—*Gazette*, weekly.
Elijay—*Courier*, weekly.
Fairburn—*Star*, weekly.
Forsyth—*Advertiser*, weekly.
Fort Valley—*Mirror*, weekly.
Franklin—*Register*, weekly.
Gainesville—*Eagle*, weekly ; *North Georgian*, weekly ; *Southron* weekly.
Greensboro—*Home Journal*, weekly ; *Herald*, weekly.
Greenville—*Vindicator*, weekly.
Griffin—*Daily News*, daily ; *Sun*, weekly.
Hamilton—*Journal*, weekly.
Hampton—*Weekly*, weekly.
Harmony Grove—*Progress*, weekly.
Hartwell—*Sun*, weekly.
Hawkinsville—*Dispatch*, weekly.
Indian Spring—*Argus*, weekly.
Irwinton—*Southerner and Appeal*, weekly.
Jefferson—*Forest News*, weekly.
Jesup—*Sentinel*, weekly.
Jonesboro—*News*, weekly.
LaGrange—*Reporter*, weekly.

Lawrenceville—*Herald*, weekly.
Lexington—*Oglethorpe Echo*, weekly.
Louisville—*News and Farmer*, weekly.
Lumpkin—*Independent*, weekly.
Macon—*Telegraph and Messenger*, daily ; *Wesleyan Christian Advocate*, weekly ; *Central Georgian*, weekly.
McVille (Telfair county)—*Southern Georgian*, weekly.
Madison—*Home Journal*, weekly.
Marietta—*Journal*, weekly ; *Field and Fireside*, weekly.
Milledgeville—*Union and Recorder*, weekly ; *Old Capital*, weekly.
Montezuma—*Weekly*, weekly.
Perry—*Home Journal*, weekly.
Newnan—*Herald*, weekly.
Quitman—*Reporter*, weekly ; *Free Press*, weekly.
Ringgold—*Catoosa Courier*, weekly.
Rome—*Bulletin*, daily ; *Tribune*, tri-weekly ; *Courier*, weekly.
Sandersville—*Herald and Georgian*, weekly ; *Courier*, weekly.
Savannah—*Morning News*, daily; *Recorder*, weekly; *Telegram*, weekly; *Times*, weekly; *Abend Zeitung*, weekly.
Social Circle—*Vidette*, weekly.
Sparta—*Times and Planter*, weekly.
Stone Mountain—*DeKalb County News*, weekly; *Spider*, weeekly.
Summerville—*Gazette*, weekly.
Swainsboro—*Herald*, weekly.
Talbotton—*Standard*, weekly; *Register*, weekly.
Thomaston—*Enterprise*, weekly.
Thomasville—*Enterprise*, weekly; *Times*, weekly.
Thomson—*McDuffie Journal*, weekly.
Toccoa—*Herald*, weekly.
Valdosta—*Times*, weekly.
Warrenton—*Clipper*, weekly.
Washington—*Gazette*, weekly.
Waynesboro—*Expositor*, weekly.
West Point—*State Line Press*, weekly.

PART II.

Sectional Divisions and County Statistics.

SHOWING THE DISTINCTIVE FEATURES OF THE VARIOUS PORTIONS OF THE STATE, ARRANGED IN DIVISIONS WITH A VIEW TO MORE INTELLIGIBLE PRESENTATION, TOGETHER WITH STATISTICAL FACTS OF PUBLIC INTEREST IN RELATION TO THE SEVERAL COUNTIES WHICH COMPOSE THEM, RESPECTIVELY.

———————

The very full information respecting the various sections and counties of the State, contained in the following pages, is condensed from answers made by a number of intelligent and responsible citizens in each county to a series of questions propounded by this Department, and designed to embrace every general and local characteristic that is of sufficient importance to interest the public. Where correspondents in the same county differ, the average of their answers is given. In order to observe greater particularity of description in this part of the *Manual*, the State has been divided into six Divisions, or Sections, instead of three, as used in Part I. It may be proper, also, to remark that the word "irreclaimable" as applied to the swamp lands of the State, is not to be received in its exact sense, but only as indicating that such lands cannot be reclaimed except at a cost which our people are at present unable to pay. The proportion of "cleared" lands, includes all that portion where the original forest has been removed, much of which, after exhaustion and abandonment, has again grown up with old field pines and other vegetation.

It is regretted that the statistics of a few of the towns are incomplete; the Commissioner has made earnest and persistent efforts with the local authorities, and others, to obtain them, but in vain.

NORTH–EAST GEORGIA.

This division embraces nineteen counties, stretching from the Savannah and Tugalo rivers in the east, to the Cohutta range of mountains in the west. It is that part of the State which possesses the greatest elevation, the average being 1,500 feet above the level of the sea. while there are peaks which rise to an elevation of near 5,000 feet. The region is metamorphic, or composed of rocks changed from their original condition by heat and pressure. The geological formations are granite, gneiss, mica, and hornblende schists; soils red and gray, resting on a basis of firm clay, usually red but sometimes yellow, white, and blue mixed with gravel, the latter chiefly on lowlands. The clay, or subsoil, is usually found from four to six inches below the surface on uplands, from one to two feet in the valleys, and from two to six feet in river bottoms. The original forest growth is, chiefly, red, black, post, and white oaks; chestnut, black-jack, hickory, short-leaf and spruce pine, cedar, dogwood, black-gum, walnut, with poplar, ash, elm, sycamore, birch, sweet-gum and white-oak on the lowlands. This is the great auriferous region of the State, the net yield of gold being equal to that of any section of the Union, California not excepted. Copper, lead, magnetic iron ore, mica, asbestus, marble, ruby, serpentine, corundum, are also found in considerable quantities, and may be mined with profit.

The lands are generally rich and productive, the yield depending wholly on the skill used in their cultivation. The staple field products are Indian corn, wheat, oats, rye, barley, clover, the various grasses, and sorghum cane, while in the southern portion of the division cotton is grown to a considerable extent. The average yield per acre. under fair cultivation, is: corn, 20 bushels; wheat 15 bushels; oats, 25 bushels; rye, 8 bushels; barley, 25 bushels, hay, from 2 to 3 tons; sorghum syrup, 75 gallons; cotton, 400 pounds in the seed. Under high culture, two, three, and sometimes four times this production is realized. Tobacco, buckwheat, and German millet can also be grown with great success. The planting and harvest times of the division are as follows: corn, planted 15th March to 15th May, gathered in fall months; wheat and other small grain sowed in October, harvested in June and July; cotton planted 15th April to 15th May, gathered in fall months; sorghum planted in April, cut in August. A very large proportion of the laborers, both farm and mine, are white; wages of former, $8 to $10 per month; of latter 75 cents to $1 per day; ordinary mechanics, $1 to $2 per day, according to skill.

The fruits best adapted to the section are, the apple, cherry, pear, grape, plum, in all its varieties, peach, gooseberry, raspberry, strawberry—the last named producing equally well in all parts of the State with like cultivation. Almost every variety of vegetables attains to great perfection.

The climate is unsurpassed on the continent for comfort and salubrity, during nine months of the year. The mean temperature in summer is 70°, Fahrenheit, in winter 35°; highest temperature 90°, lowest 8°—periods of greater heat and cold being exceptional. Snow falls usually from two to three times during the winter season, especially in the northernmost counties, to a depth varying from two inches to six inches. In the southern tier of counties, there are occasional winters without a fall of snow.

Springs and running streams abound in all parts of the district; water powers unsurpassed; spring and well water freestone, and not excelled in any country. Mineral springs—sulphur or chalybeate—abound in nearly all the counties of the district. That portion of it—the eastern—to which railroad transportation has been opened, is annually visited by thousands, many of whom spend the entire summer and part of autumn at its watering places and pleasant villages. It may be said of this, and indeed of all other sections of the State, that the people are anxious for new settlers. and are ready to give a cordial welcome to honest and industrious immigrants from all countries, including our own. Lands can be bought at low prices and on favorable terms, as regards the payments—in the mountains from $1 to $5 per acre, and in the valleys and lower portions of the district from $5 to $10 per acre. The average price of farm stock varies but little in the

State, and may be stated as follows: milch cows, $15 to $20; sheep $1.50 to $2; brood sows, $5 to $8; horses and mules $75 to $100.

COUNTIES.

Bank—Population, in 1870, the date of the last census, 4,973—4,052 white, 921 black. Two per cent. of county too mountainous for cultivation, thirty-three per cent. of tillable land cleared, seventy-five per cent. field labor performed by whites, twenty-nine public free schools for whites and four for blacks, Baptist churches ten, Methodist eight, Presbyterian three.

Homer, the capital town, is 10 miles from Air-Line Railroad, has a population of 110—100 whites 10 blacks—20 private dwellings, 1 hotel, 3 churches, 1 school with 30 scholars, 2 dry goods stores, 1 grocery store, 1 physician, 2 lawyers.

Dawson—Population in 1870, 4,369—4,032 white, 337 black. Ten per cent. of county too mountainous for culture, of tillable land 30 per cent. cleared, gold mined to considerable extent with good success, pounding mill in county, copper and silver also discovered. 90 per cent. field labor done by whites, public free schools 24 for whites, 2 for blacks, several private schools. Baptist churches 17, Methodist 14, Universalist 1.

Dawsonville, the capital town, is 23 miles from Air-Line Railroad, has a population of 225—200 white, 25 black, 50 private dwellings, 1 hotel, 3 churches, 1 school with 40 scholars, 3 dry goods stores, 1 grocery store, 2 physicians, 1 lawyer.

Fannin—Population, in 1870, 5,429—5,285 white, 144 black; 20 per cent. of area too mountainous for cultivation, 1½ per cent. irreclaimable swamp, 40 per cent. of tillable land cleared, 99½ per cent. of farm laborers white; the minerals are gold, copper, iron, mica, marble, limestone; copper mines in western part of county very rich, marble in great abundance and of many varieties; 34 public free schools for whites, 1 for blacks; 16 Methodist churches, 15 Baptist; 1 iron furnace, 12 operatives; 1 wool-carding machine, flour and lumber mills.

Morganton, the capital town, on line of survey Marietta & North Georgia Railroad, has 107 inhabitants—103 white, 4 black, 22 private dwellings, 1 hotel, 1 church, 1 school with 50 pupils, 3 dry goods stores, 1 grocery store, 5 physicians, 3 lawyers.

Forsyth—Population, in 1870, 7,983—6,862 white, 1,121 black; 5 per cent. too mountainous for tillage; 50 per cent. tillable land cleared; 90 per cent. field labor performed by whites; minerals—gold, copper, iron ore, but limited in extent; public free schools 51 for whites, 9 for blacks; Baptist churches 15, Methodist 10.

Cumming, the capital town, is 12 miles from Air-Line Railroad, 40 miles from Atlanta, has population 400—385 white, 15 black, sixty private dwellings, 2 hotels, 2 churches, 1 school, 60 scholars, 1 weekly newspaper, 8 mixed stores, 1 drug store, 3 physicians, 6 lawyers.

Franklin—Population, in 1870, 7,893—6,034 white, 1,859 black; 5 per cent. of county too mountainous for tillage; 40 per cent. tillable land cleared; 75 per cent. field labor performed by whites; public free schools

36 for whites, 4 for blacks, besides private schools; Baptist churches 20, Methodist 15, Presbyterian 4; 5 wool-carding machines, 1 cotton factory.

Carnesville, the capital town, is 18 miles from Air-Line Railroad, same distance from market town, has population 730—700 white, 30 black, 165 private dwellings, 1 hotel, 2 churches, 1 school with 76 pupils, 4 mixed stores, 2 drug stores, 1 weekly newspaper, 5 physicians, 3 lawyers.

Gilmer—Population, in 1870, 6,644 –6,527 white, 117 black; 33 per cent. of county too mountainous for cultivation; 33 per cent. of tillable land cleared; minerals—gold. copper, iron, marble, slate; mining limited in extent; large stratum of limestone running along side of iron belt; 35 public free schools for whites, 1 for blacks, besides private schools; 23 Baptist churches, 20 Methodist.

Ellijay, the capital town, is 40 miles from Western & Atlantic Railroad, has a population 203—200 whites, 3 blacks, 35 private dwellings, 1 hotel, 3 churches, 1 high school with 75 scholars, 1 weekly newspaper, 3 mixed stores, 3 physicians. 2 lawyers.

Gwinnett—Population, in 1870, 12,431—10,272 white, 2,159 black; 5 per cent. of county too mountainous for tillage; of tillable land 58 per cent. cleared; some gold, but not mined of late years; 75 per cent. field labor performed by whites; public free schools, 52 for whites, 13 for blacks, besides private schools; 20 Baptist churches, 15 Methodist, 5 Episcopal. several Presbyterian.

Lawrenceville, the capital town, is 8 miles from Air-Line Railroad 30 miles from Atlanta, has a population of 600—400 white, 200 black, 175 private dwellings, 1 hotel, 4 churches, 2 schools with 80 scholars, 1 weekly newspaper, 3 dry goods stores, 6 grocery stores, 3 physicians, 6 lawyers.

Habersham—Population, in 1870, 6,322—5,373 white, 949 black; 10 per cent. of county too mountainous for cultivation; 30 per cent. tillable land cleared; minerals—gold, iron, asbestus; 90 per cent. field laborers white; 30 public schools for whites, 3 for blacks; Baptist churches 24, Methodist 8, Presbyterian 2, Episcopal 1.

Clarkesville, the capital town, is 7½ miles from Air-Line Railroad, 87 from Atlanta, has a population of 290—218 white, 72 black, 71 private dwellings, 2 hotels, 3 churches, 2 schools with 40 scholars, 8 dry goods stores, 4 grocery stores, 2 physicians, 4 lawyers.

Toccoa City, on Air-Line Railroad, 92 miles from Atlanta, has a population of 900—600 white, 300 black, 125 private dwellings, 2 hotels, 5 churches, 3 schools with 100 scholars, 1 weekly newspaper, 24 mixed stores, 3 physicians, 3 lawyers.

Mount Airy, on same road, 9 miles from Clarkesville, 80 miles from Atlanta, bids fair to become a place of note; is most elevated town and railroad point in the South, being 1,610 feet above the sea, and 560 feet above Atlanta; has now 86 inhabitants—60 white, 26 black, 14 private dwellings, 1 large and splendid hotel, 2 churches, 1 school with 20 scholars, 4 mixed stores, 1 physician.

Hall—Population, in 1870, 9,607—8,317 white, 1,290 black; 10 per cent. of county too mountainous for tillage; 30 per cent. tillable land cleared;

minerals—gold. (large amounts invested in working) copper, silver, iron, lead, manganese, mica, asbestus, most of precious stones, including diamonds; 90 per cent. miners and field laborers white; public free schools, 57 for whites, 5 for blacks; 6 Baptist churches. 7 Methodist, 2 Presbyterian, 1 Episcopal.

Gainesville, the capital town, is on Air-Line Railroad, 54 miles from Atlanta, has a population of 2,500—2,000 white, 500 black, 500 private dwellings, 4 large hotels, 1 bank 4 churches, 5 schools with 400 scholars, 3 weekly newspapers, 15 dry goods stores, 6 grocery stores, 6 physicians, 15 lawyers, 2 dentists.

HART—Population, in 1870, 6,783—4,841 white, 1,942 black; 30 per cent. of tillable land cleared; minerals—gold, copper, black lead; several mines gold worked with great success before the war, no operations now; 70 per cent. field laborers white; public free schools, 29 for whites, 6 for blacks; Baptist churches 11, Methodist 9, Presbyterian 2. Seceding Baptist 2,; 1 factory for cotton yarns, 30 hands.

Hartwell, the capital town, is 30 miles from Air-Line Railroad at Toccoa City, 40 miles from Athens, has a population of 350—300 white, 50 black, 50 private dwellings, 1 hotel, 2 churches, 1 school with 75 scholars, 1 weekly newspaper, 7 dry goods stores, 3 grocery stores, 4 physicians, 7 lawyers, 1 dentist.

JACKSON—Population, in 1870, 11,181—7,471 white. 3,710 black; whole area tillable; 44 per cent. cleared; gold, silver, mica, copper found, but not sufficient for mining; 66 per cent. farm laborers white; public free schools, 49 for whites, 8 for blacks; Baptist churches 17, Methodist 15, Presbyterian 5, several Christian and Universalist; furniture, wagons, buggies, manufactured to some extent.

Jefferson, the capital town, is 18 miles from Athens, the market town, 9 miles from North Western Railroad. (Further details not reported.)

LUMPKIN—Population, in 1870, 5,161—4,699 white, 462 black; 25 per cent. of area too mountainous for tillage; 60 per cent. of tillable land cleared; 90 per cent. of farm laborers white; is leading gold mining county of State; has 20 pounding mills with 220 stamps—annual yield very large; copper, iron and mica also exist, but not mined; larger part of population engaged in mining; has 50 public free schools for whites. 4 for blacks; prevailing religious denominations Methodist, Baptist. Presbyterian ; flour and lumber mills abundant.

Dahlonega. the capital town, is 24 miles from Gainesville and Atlanta & Charlotte Air-Line Railroad, has 600 inhabitants—500 white, 100 black. 4 churches, is site of North Georgia Agricultural College, with 250 pupils, has 8 dry goods stores; 6 grocery stores, 100 private dwellings, 3 hotels, 2 physicians, 4 lawyers.

MADISON—Population, in 1870, 5 227—3,646 white, 1,581 black ; 5 per cent. of county too broken for tillage: 1 per cent. too swampy ; 31 per cent. of tillable land cleared; gold in deposit and iron ore exist, but not worked in many years; 65 per cent. of farm laborers white; Baptist churches 10 Methodist 6, Presbyterian 3, Primitive Baptist 4.

Danielsville, the capital town, is 15 miles distant from Athens, the market town. (Further details not reported.)

MILTON—Population, in 1870, 4,584—3,118 white, 466 black; 10 per cent. of county too broken, or too swampy, for successful tillage; 40 per cent. of tillable land cleared; 75 per cent. of field labor performed by whites; 20 free public schools for whites, 4 for blacks; religious denominations almost wholly Baptists and Meth dists.

Alpharetta, the capital town, is 14 miles from Air-Line Railroad and 30 miles from Atlanta, has a population of 285—275 white, 12 black; 30 private dwellings, 1 hotel, 1 church, 1 school with 45 scholars, 2 dry goods stores, 1 grocery store, 2 drug stores, 3 physicians, 4 lawyers, 1 dentist.

PICKENS—Population, in 1870, 5,317—5,188 white, 120 black; 19 per cent. of county too m untaino.s for cultivation; 33 per cent. of tillable land c'ear d; go'd, copper, iron, nickel, marble, exist i. considerable quantities, but not min d at presen ; 90 per cent. of field laborers whitr; 25 public free schools for whites, 1 for blacks; Bap ist churches 18. Methodist 3, Presbyterian 1, some Bible Christians; 1 cotton mill with 40 operatives.

Jasper, the capi'al town, is 50 miles from Air-Line Railroad immediately on line of survey Marietta & North Georgia Railroad, and 60 miles from A.lanta, the market town. (Further details not reported.)

RABUN—Population, in 1870, 3,256—3,137 white, 119 black; 81 per cent. of c un y to m u?tainous for cultivation : 70 per cent. of tillable land cleared; mines of gold a d asbestrs being worked with success; copper and iron ore discovered; 92 per cent. farm labor performed by whit s; 22 public free schools, all for whites; Baptist chu: chss 12, Methodist 7; 1 wool-carding machine in operation.

Clayton, the capital town, is 27 miles from Air Line Railroad and Toccoa the market town, has a population of 137—120 white, 17 black; 30 private dwellings, 1 hotel, 2 churches, 1 school with 36 scholars, 4 mixed stores, no lawyers, physicians, dentists, or bar-rooms.

TOWNS—Populatio , in 1870, 2,780—2,623 white, 155 black; 50 per cent. of county too mountainous for culture; 75 per cent. of tillable land cleared; gold and copper exist, but no great amount of mining; many of the p e-cious stones in more or less quantities; 98 per cent. of farm laborers white; public free schools, for w..ites 13, for blacks 1; Baptist churches 10, Methodist 4.

Hiawassee, the capital town, is 40 miles from a r.ilroad, 54 from Gainesville, 1(8 from Atlanta; has a population of 60, all white; 9 private dwellings, 1 hotel, no church, 1 school, 2 mixed stores, 1 physic'an, 2 lawyers.

UNION—Population, in 1870, 5,267—5,153 white, 114 black; 25 per cent. of county too mountainous for tillage; 25 per cent. of tillable land cleared; gold, copper, iron, red and brown hematite, corundum exist in considerable quantities, also mica; only gold being mined successfully; 95 per cent. of miners and farm hands white; public free schools, 25 for whites, 1 for blacks; Baptist churches 12, Methodist 12, Presbyterian 2.

Blairsville, the capital town, is 52 miles from Gainesville, the market town, 106 f.om Atlanta, has a population of 131—120 white, 11 black, 1 hotel, 26 private dwellings, 2 churches, 1 school, 3 mixed stores, 2 physicians, 2 lawyers.

WHITE—Population, in 1870, 4,606—4,042 white, 564 black ; 10 per cent. too mountainous for cultivation ; 30 per cent. of tillable land cleared, gold and iron exist to a large extent, the former mined with much success and to considerable extent ; 99 per cent. of laborers white ; 21 free public schools for whites, 3 for blacks; 8 Baptist churches, 10 Methodist, 1 Episcopal, 1 Christian : gold mills and liquor distilleries the only manufactories.

Cleveland, the capital town, is 18 miles from the Air-Line Railroad, 25 from Gainesville, the market town of the county, has a population of 175—150 white, 25 black, 1 hotel, 36 private dwellings, 3 churches, 1 school with 100 scholars, 3 dry goods stores, 4 grocery stores, 2 physicians, 5 lawyers, 3 dentists.

NORTH-WEST GEORGIA.

This division embraces fourteen counties, and extends from the Cohutta Mountains and Chattahoochee Ridge to the eastern boundary of Alabama. It differs, in several important respects, from the North-eastern division. It is less mountainous, and, consequently, a greater portion of its area is susceptible of cultivation. Its average elevation above the sea is only 750 feet, or about 50 per cent. less than that of Northeast Georgia. Its geological ages are Silurian, Devonian (so called from their identity with those of Wales and Devonshire), and, in the extreme northwest, Carboniferous. The characteristic minerals are limestone, slate, iron ores, coal, manganese, sandstone, baryta, some gold, all of which, except the last, are found in great quantities. Several valuable veins and gravelly deposits of gold have been developed and worked, with handsome returns.

The immense coal beds described in the chapter on minerals lie in the northwestern counties of this division, to-wit : Dade, Walker and Chattooga. The supply seems to be inexhaustible ; the mines are reached by railroads which connect with main trunks, and in the immediate vicinity are immense deposits of best iron ore.

The soils are calcareous and argillaceous ; clay, red and yellow. In all other respects our description of the natural conditions and capabilities of North-east Georgia will apply to this division, with the single exception of temperature, the difference in elevation being accompanied by the usual variations of heat and cold. The productions are, in all respects, the same.

In one or two respects, this division enjoys peculiar advantages over its eastern neighbor. It has not only a larger area of tillable land, but much greater proportion of valley and river bottom. Its facilities for transportation are also greater, the Western and Atlantic Railroad traversing its centre from the northern to the southern boundary. while tributary roads supply a good portion of the country to the right and left of the main line.

The whole of North Georgia is admirably adapted to stock-raising. The mountains afford abundant pasturage for cattle, sheep, hogs, goats, etc., which are required to be fed only a few months in the year, while the grains and grasses are produced in the greatest abundance for that purpose.

COUNTIES.

BARTOW—Population in 1870, 16,566—11,840 whites, 4.719 blacks; 25 per cent. of county too mountainous for cultivation, 1½ per cent. irreclaimable swamp, 50 per cent. of tillable land cleared; minerals—gold, iron, manganese, baryta, slate in abundance and of best quality; gold mining confined to surface washing and very profitable; iron mined on a large scale, and much ore shipped to Chattanooga and other points; one furnace now turning out 70 tons pig per day; 75 per cent. field labor performed by whites; 67 public free schools for whites, 23 for blacks, besides two large private schools; religious denominations chiefly Baptist, Methodist, and Episcopal; manufactories—iron foundries, lime and cement works, carriage and wagon factories, flour, corn and saw mills.

Cartersville, the capital town. is at junction of two railroads, 12 miles from a navigable stream, and 47 miles from Atlanta; has a population of 4,000—2.500 whites, 1,500 blacks, 350 private dwellings, 2 hotels, 6 churches, 3 schools, 1 weekly newspaper, 15 dry goods stores, 20 grocery stores, 13 physicians, 20 lawyers, 3 dentists.

Adairsville, on Western and Atlantic Railroad, 20 miles from Cartersville, 67 miles from Atlanta, has a population of 325—300 white, 25 black, 75 private dwellings, 1 hotel, 1 church, 1 school with 50 scholars, 6 dry goods stores, 4 grocery stores, 2 physicians.

Kingston is on the Western and Atlantic Railroad. at the terminus of the Rome Railroad, 60 miles from Atlanta, 18 miles from Rome, has about 600 inhabitants—400 white, 200 black; 4 mixed stores, 1 drug store; assessed value of real estate, $75,000.

CATOOSA—Population in 1870, 4,409—3,793 white, 616 black, 10 per cent. of county too mountainous for cultivation, of tillable land 43 per cent. cleared; iron ores of best quality abound, but not mined; 85 per cent. of field laborers white; 21 public free schools for whites, 2 for blacks; Baptist churches 7, Methodist 7, Presbyterian 1; manufactories of lime, fertilizers, 3 large merchant flour mills, corn and saw mills.

Ringgold, the capital town, is on the Western and Atlantic Railroad, 114 miles from Atlanta, 24 from Chattanooga, (details not reported).

CHATTOOGA—Population in 1870, 6,902—5,309 white, 1,503 black; 21 per cent. of area too mountainous for tillage, of tillable land 55 per cent. cleared; coal and iron ore abound in county and are of best quality; 80 per cent. field laborers white; 29 free public schools; Baptist churches 11, Methodist 8, Presbyterian 6, besides colored churches; 1 cotton mill 10,000 spindles and 300 operatives, 12 tanyards, flour, corn and saw mills.

Summerville, the capital town, 25 miles from Western and Atlantic Railroad, and Dalton the market town, has a population of 400—300 white, 100 black, 97 private dwellings, 1 hotel, 3 churches, 2 schools with 50 scholars, 1 weekly newspaper, 4 dry goods stores, 1 grocery store, 3 physicians, 4 lawyers.

CHEROKEE—Population in 1870, 10,399—9,117 white, 1,281 black; 15 per cent. of county too mountainous for cultivation, 45 per cent of tillable land cleared; gold, copper, iron principal metals—3 large gold mines now worked with good success, and a number of rich veins recently opened; Canton copper mines worked with profit; silver and lead exist in small quantities; 78 per cent. field laborers white; 56 public free schools for whites, 7 for blacks, also private schools; Methodist churches 25, Baptist 25, Presbyterian 2, Universalist 2; 2 cotton factories, 1 threshing machine factory, tanyards, wagon factories, saw and grist mills.

Canton, the capital town, on located line of Marietta and North Georgia Railroad, unfinished, is 22 miles from Marietta, on the Western and Atlantic Railroad, the market town, 40 miles from Atlanta, has a population of 330—300 white, 30 black, 55 private dwellings, 2 churches, 1 school with 40 pupils, 1 weekly newspaper, 4 mixed stores, 2 physicians, 9 lawyers.

Cobb.—Population in 1870, 13,814—10,593 white, 3,217 black; entire county considered tillable, 65 per cent. cleared; principal minerals, gold, copper, iron ores of superior quality and abundant, sulphurets, asbestus; but little mining at present; 60 per cent. of farm labor done by whites, 59 public free schools for whites, 39 for blacks, besides high schools; Baptist churches 23, Methodist 15, Presbyterian 6, Episcopal 1, Christian 1. Manufactories—Roswell Cotton Mills, 250 operatives; Willeo Cotton Mills, 75; Concord Woolen Mills, 31; Laurel Woolen Mills, 35; Marietta Paper Mills, 20; chair factory, 25; Withers' Iron Foundry, 5; also, 2 large Merchant flouring mills, with numerous corn, flour and saw mills.

Marietta, the capital town, on Western and Atlantic Railroad, 20 miles from Atlanta, has a population of 2,512—1,395 white, 1,117 black, 300 private dwellings, 1 first-class hotel, 1 bank, 6 churches, 8 schools with 250 scholars, 2 weekly newspapers, 10 dry goods stores, 20 grocery stores, 4 physicians, 14 lawyers, 3 dentists.

Dade—Population in 1870, 3,033—2,788 white, 245 black; 20 per cent. of county too mountainous for tillage, 25 per cent. of tillable land cleared; of minerals, iron and coal exist in exhaustless deposits and are extensively worked—one company, the Dade Coal Company, getting out 15,000 bushels per day; also, coke and iron furnaces, one of the latter, at Rising Fawn, turning out 40 tons pig iron per day; 80 per cent. of field laborers white; 14 public free schools for whites, 1 for blacks; 3 Baptist churches, 14 Methodist, 1 Presbyterian, 1 Christian, 1 Second Advent.

Trenton, the capital town, is on Alabama and Chattanooga Railroad, 18 miles from Chattanooga, 15 miles from Tennessee River, has 125 inhabitants —115 white, 10 black, 30 private dwellings, 1 hotel, 2 churches, 1 school with 80 scholars, 2 dry goods stores, 1 grocery store, 1 physician, 3 lawyers.

Clover Dale has 50 whites, 10 blacks, 1 church, 1 school with 40 pupils, 1 dry goods store.

Floyd—Population in 1870, 17,230—11,473 white, 5,753 black; 33 per cent. of county too mountainous for tillage; of tillable land 65 per cent. cleared; iron ore, marble, slate, principal minerals; 53 per cent. of field laborers white; 72 free public schools for whites, 25 for blacks; 20 Baptist churches, 30 Methodist, 4 Presbyterian, 1 Episcopal, 1 Roman Catholic; manufactories of iron, nails, car wheels, ploughs, staves, hollow ware, commercial fertilizers, numerous flour, corn and saw mills.

Rome. the capital town, is on two railroads and navigable stream, is a market town of county, and 78½ miles from Atlanta by rail; 4 banks; (details not reported).

Cave Spring is a village of 800 inhabitants—650 white, 150 black, has 115 private dwellings, 1 hotel, 7 churches, 5 schools with 245 scholars, 1 weekly newspaper, 4 dry goods stores, 4 grocery stores, 5 physicians, no lawyers nor dentists ; is seat of State Deaf and Dumb Institute.

GORDON—Population in 1870, 9,268—7,726 white, 1,536 black ; 20 per cent. of county too mountainous for tillage, 8 per cent. irreclaimable swamp, of tillable land 75 per cent. is cleared; iron ore, slate, tripoli the principal minerals, but not worked to great extent; 70 per cent. of field laborers white; 43 free public schools for whites, 8 for blacks ; Baptist and Methodist principal religious denominations.

Calhoun, the capital town, on Western and Atlantic Railroad, 2 miles from navigable stream, 80 miles from Atlanta, has a population of 1,000 –800 white, 200 black, 200 private dwelllings, 1 hotel, 2 churches, 2 schools with 100 scholars, 1 weekly newspaper, 5 dry goods stores, 8 grocery stores, 4 physicians, 12 lawyers, 1 dentist.

Resaca, on Western and Atlantic Railroad, 85 miles from Atlanta, on Oostanaula River, village of 210 inhabitants—200 white, 10 black, 25 private dwellings, 1 hotel, 2 churches, 1 school with 35 scholars, 5 dry goods stores, 1 grocery store, 2 physicians.

HARALSON—Population in 1870, 4,004—3,685 white, 319 black ; 7½ per cent. of county too mountainous for cultivation, 3 per cent. irreclaimable swamp, of tillable land 27 per cent. cleared; principal minerals, copper and gold ; 6 shafts of copper now worked with success, gold washings to a limited extent; 92½ per cent. of farm laborers white ; 21 free public schools for whites, 1 for blacks ; 10 Baptist churches, 8 Methodist, 6 Primitive Baptist, 1 Christian ; 1 wool factory.

Buchanan, the capital town, is 20 miles from Cartersville and Van Wert Railroad, 40 miles from Rome, 55 miles from Atlanta, (details not reported).

MURRAY—Population in 1870, 6,500—5,743 white, 757 black ; 10 per cent. of county too mountainous for tillage ; 50 per cent of tillable land cleared ; gold, silver, lead exist in small quantities but none worked ; also, slate and soapstone, the latter being mined for lubricating purposes ; 80 per cent. of farm laborers white ; 30 free public schools for whites, 3 for blacks ; 14 Baptist churches, 12 Methodist, 2 Presbyterian ; flour, corn and saw mills only manufacturing establishments.

Spring Place—the capital town, is 11 miles from Dalton, the market town, on Western and Atlantic Railroad, 15 miles from a navigable stream, has a population of 259—250 white, 9 black, 42 private dwellings, 1 hotel, 3 churches, 1 school with 30 scholars, 3 dry goods stores, 2 grocery stores, 1 drug store, 3 physicians, 3 lawyers.

PAULDING—Population in 1870, 7,639—7,083 white, 556 black ; 8 per cent. of county too mountainous or rocky for cultivation, of tillable land, 53 per cent. cleared ; minerals, gold, iron, copper, asbestus; little mining owing to want of capital ; 90 per cent. of farm laborers white ; 38 free public schools, all for whites; Baptist churches 25, Methodist 24; 1 wool-carding machine, 1 shingle machine, only manufactories.

Dallas, the capital town, 16 miles from Acworth, on Western & Atlantic Railroad, market town; 30 miles from Rome and navigable stream, has a population of 177—165 white, 12 black, 30 private dwellings, 1 hotel, 3 churches, 1 school with 30 scholars, 2 dry goods stores, 3 grocery stores, 2 physicians, 6 lawyers.

PoLK—Population, in 1870, 7,822—5.244 white, 2,578 black; 14 per cent. of county too mountainous for successful tillage; 44 per cent. of tillable land cleared; pine timber abundant, and of fine quality; principal minerals—slate, iron, limestone, marble, ochre, manganese; Rockmart slate quarries yield 10 squares per day; Ætna iron furnace 18 tons pig iron per day, Cherokee furnace 25 tons; 57½ per cent. of field laborers white; 30 public free schools for whites, 6 for blacks; Baptist churches 12, Methodist 11, Presbyterian 2, Christian 1; manufactories of slate 60 hands, iron 300 hands, lumber 50, shoes 10, leather 6.

Cedar Town, the capital town and market, is 7 miles from Selma, Rome & Dalton Railroad, 20 miles from Coosa river at Rome, 10 miles from Cherokee Railroad, while 2 projected roads cross at the town; population 900—600 white, 300 black, 130 private dwellings, 2 hotels, 5 churches, 4 schools with 237 scholars, 2 weekly newspapers, 8 dry goods stores, 7 grocery stores, 2 drug stores, 8 physicians, 11 lawyers.

WALKER—Population, in 1870, 9,925—8,396 white, 1,529 black; 36½ per cent. of county too mountainous for cultivation; 64 per cent. of tillable land cleared; principal minerals—coal and iron in great abundance in western part of county, but not mined to any great extent for want of transportation; marble and limestone also exist in large quantities; 87 per cent. of farm laborers white; 42 public free schools for whites, 4 for blacks; Baptist churches 23, Methodist 20, Presbyterian 2, Bible Christian 1, Second Advent 1, Universalist 1; no manufactories worthy of note.

LaFayette, the capital town, is 20 miles from a railroad, 25 from Chattanooga (the market town) and Tennessee river. 12 miles from Tryon Factory, usual market for cotton; has a population of 200 whites and 60 blacks, 50 private dwellings, 1 hotel, 3 churches, 3 schools with 30 pupils, 1 weekly newspaper, 5 dry goods stores. 2 grocery stores, 1 drug store, 2 physicians, 3 lawyers, and 1 dentist.

WHITEFIELD—Population, in 1870, 10,117—8,606 white, 1,511 black; 10 per cent. of the county too mountainous for tillage; 35 per cent of tillable land cleared; iron ore of various kinds abundant, also limestone; tripoli, a bituminous shale, exists in this and in Floyd, and some other counties, which is combustible and yields oil, consequently sometimes mistaken for coal; 45 free public schools for whites, 7 for blacks; 15 Baptist churches, 17 Methodist, 4 Presbyterian, 1 Episcopal, 1 Roman Catholic, 1 Christian; manufactories—of furniture 15 hands, iron foundry 5 hands, shoe factory 6, tannery 8; 1 flouring mill 2-run stones, several lumber mills; 82½ per cent. of field laborers white.

Dalton, the capital town, on Western & Atlantic Railroad, and terminus
5

of East Tennessee & Georgia Railroad and Selma, Rome & Dalton Railroad, 100 miles from Atlanta, 38 from Chattanooga and Tennessee river, has a population of 4,000—3,500 white, 500 black, 700 private dwellings, 2 hotels, 1 bank, 11 churches, 11 schools with 400 scholars, 2 weekly newspapers, 10 dry goods stores, 15 grocery stores, 2 drug stores, 9 physicians, 16 lawyers, 2 dentists.

Tunnel Hill, on Western & Atlantic Railroad, 7 miles from Dalton, has 275 inhabitants—250 white, 25 black, 50 private dwellings, 1 hotel, 3 churches, 1 school with 75 scholars, 3 mixed stores, 2 drug stores, 3 physicians, 2 lawyers, 1 dentist.

MIDDLE GEORGIA.

This division embraces thirty-nine counties, and has an area of about 15,000 square miles. It extends across the State from the Savannah river in the east, to the Chattahoochee river in the west. Its southern border may be described with tolerable accuracy by a line from Augusta through Macon to Columpus. It is marked by the head of navigation of the principal rivers. The northern border may be described by a line running through Athens and Atlanta. It is about one hundred miles in width. Its average elevation is 750 feet. The entire region is metamorphic; its rocks, granite, gneiss, mica, quartzites, hydro-mica schist, with some limestone and soapstone. These rocks all extend from the northeast to the southwest, and are crossed frequently at right angles by trap dykes. Its chief minerals are gold, copper, lead, asbestus, graphite, chromic iron, serpentine and soapstone. Gold is found in districts wide apart, and has been worked with satisfactory profit in a few localities, more especially in McDuffie, Lincoln, Wilkes and Carroll. Asbestus is also mined to some extent. The original forest growth consists of red, post, Spanish and white oaks, and black-jack, hickory, short-leaf pine, with some long-leaf on its southern border; poplar, dogwood, elm, chestnut, maple, beech, birch, ash, black locust, sweet and black gums, walnut and some cedar. This division has three varieties of soil—red or clay, gray and gravelly, and light and sandy, the last named being limited in extent and confined to the long-leaf pine localities on the southern border. The two former possess great productiveness and durability. After the coast country, they were the first settled, and Middle Georgia has continued to be the most populous division of the State. While the lowlands are of the best quality, the uplands are unsurpassed in fertility and luxuriance of forest growth by those of any country. A very large proportion of the lands has suffered temporary exhaustion by injudicious culture which claimed everything from the soil and returned nothing. This ruinous practice is fast giving way to a more enlightened and economical system. It has been ascertained that no soils on the continent are more susceptible of recuperation and respond so bountifully to generous treatment. The abandoned fields, grown up in stunted pines, and for twenty or forty years considered useful only as pasturage, have been restored to cultivation, and are now among the most productive lands of the State. The staple field products are cotton, corn, oats and wheat, while all the grains and grasses, and even tobacco, may be grown successfully. The average yields with ordinary culture, are: Cotton, 550 pounds, in seed, per acre; corn, 12 bushels; wheat, 8 bushels; oats, 25 bushels; barley, 30 bushels; rye, 8 bushels; sweet potatoes, 100 bushels; field peas with corn, 5 bushels. Ground peas, chufas, pumpkins, and, indeed, almost every field product, are successfully cultivated. Very many farmers double the above averages year after year, whilst under high culture the product is multiplied four or five times, as will be seen in the chapter on that subject. About 75 per cent. of the farm laborers of this division are negroes, and the average wages are $8.00 per month and rations. Wages of ordinary mechanics vary from $1.50 to $3.00 per day, according to skill. The planting and harvest periods of leading products are : Cotton, April, September to December; corn, March, October; wheat, October and November, May and early June; other fall grains harvested same time; those sowed in February and March harvested in June. The fruits to which the section is best adapted are the peach, fig, apple, pear, strawberry, raspberry, melons of all kinds. The peach attains here, and in South-west Georgia, its greatest perfection, and immense quantities are raised for export, both in their natural and dried state; the same may be said of the apple and blackberry, though the latter is a spontaneous growth and yields abundantly in a wild state. Almost every other variety of fruit known in the Southern States thrives well in this division. The table vegetables are all grown successfully, the hardier varieties the year round. The climate is a happy medium between those of Southern and Northern Georgia, and, in healthfulness, equal to that of any part of the world. There is much uniformity of temperature, sudden rises and falls occurring but rarely. The mean annual temperature is 60° to 64°. Snow falls about once in three years, the depth varying from 1½ to 4 inches Every portion of the division abounds in running streams, while the spring and well waters are excellent. The difference in elevation between the Northern and the Southern portions of the division being from 650 to 700 feet, the water-powers are probably unequalled by those of any similar area on the continent. It would be difficult to fix a limit to its manufacturing facilities in this respect. The society is good, and the people educated and refined. Immigration is desired and good lands can be bought on liberal terms at from $4.00 to $10.00 per acre. The mineral springs are few, but for curative powers are unsurpassed in the Union. The Indian Spring, in Butts county, and the Warm and Sulphur Springs, in Meriwether, are famous resorts of invalids, and enjoy a deserved popularity.

COUNTIES.

BALDWIN—Population in 1870, 10,618—3,844 white, 6,744 black; 62 per cent. of tillable land cleared, 90 per cent. of field laborers black ; 18 free public schools for whites, 16 for blacks ; Baptist churches 4 Methodist 5, Presbyterian 1, Episcopal 1, Roman Catholic 1—all for whites; blacks have about same number; one large cotton factory in county.

Milledgeville, the capital town, is on south bank of Oconee river, is market town for the county, at crossing of two railroads; has a population of 4,000—1828 white, 2,172 black; 500 private dwellings, 1 hotel, 1 bank, 9 churches, 7 schools with 145 scholars, 2 weekly newspapers, 9 dry goods stores, 22 grocery stores, 2 drug stores, 4 physicians, 7 lawyers and 2 dentists.

BUTTS—Population in 1870, 6,941—3,496 white, 3,445 black ; 1 per cent. of county too broken for cultivation, 2 per cent. irreclaimable swamp, 45 per cent. of tillable land cleared; 50 per cent. of field laborers white; 17 free public schools for whites, 8 for blacks; Baptist churches 9, Methodist 6, Presbyterian, 1; flour and saw mills abundant, and only manufactories of the county. The famous Indian Spring is in this county.

Jackson, the county site, is 20 miles from a railroad and market town, 45 from head of navigation on Ocmulgee river, has 400 inhabitants—250 white, 150 black; 40 private dwellings, 1 hotel, 2 churches, 1 school with 40 scholars, 1 weekly newspaper, 3 dry goods stores, 1 grocery store, 1 drug store, 4 physicians, 3 lawyers, 1 dentist.

CAMPBELL—Population in 1870, 9,175—6,589 white, 2.587 black; 63 per cent. of tillable land cleared; 24 free public schools for whites, 8 for blacks; Baptist churches 18, Methodist 8, Lutheran 1, Protestant Methodist 2. Blacks have 6 Baptist and 8 Methodist churches; wagon and buggy factories, flour and corn mills, the only manufacturing interests.

Fairburn, the capital town, is on the Atlanta and West Point railroad, 19 miles from Atlanta, the market town; has 550 inhabitants—400 white, 150 black; 100 private dwellings, 1 hotel, 6 churches, 1 school with 80 scholars, 7 dry goods stores, 8 grocery stores, 1 drug store, 3 physicians, 8 lawyers, 1 dentist.

Campbellton, the old capital has a population of 66—39 white, 27 black; 15 private dwellings, 1 hotel, 4 churches, 1 school with 21 scholars, one dry goods store, 2 grocery stores, 1 drug store, 3 physicians.

CARROLL—Population in 1870, 11,782—10,473 white, 1,309 black; only 15 per cent. of tillable land cleared; entire under strata of county mineral, several gold mines have been extensively and successfully worked, copper and manganese also exist in quantities to justify mining; 80 per cent. of field labor performed by whites; 63 free public schools for whites, 10 for blacks, besides private schools; Baptist churches 31, Methodist 35, Presbyterian 3, Christian 2; 1 cotton factory, 1 paper mill, numerous flour, corn and lumber mills.

Carrollton, the capital town, on Savannah, Griffin and North Alabama Railroad, is market town for the county; has 1,325 inhabitants—950 white, 375 black; 200 private dwellings, 2 hotels, 5 churches, 4 schools with 124 pupils, 1 weekly newspaper, 12 dry goods stores, 4 grocery stores, 2 drug stores, 6 physicians, 12 lawyers, 1 dentist.

CLARKE—Population, in 1870, 12,941—6,488 white, 6,453 black; 78 per cent. of original forest felled; 33 per cent of it in cultivation; 70 per cent. of farm laborers black; State University located in the county; 2 female high schools; 19 public free schools for whites, 17 for blacks; 9 Baptist churches, 6 Methodist, 2 Episcopal, 2 Presbyterian, 1 Roman Catholic, 1 Jewish synagogue; the county has 3 cotton factories and 1 paper mill, employing together 200 hands; 1 iron foundry and machine shop, 20 hands; 1 bobbin mill, 4 hands; 1 door, sash and blind factory, 20 hands; 1 planing mill, besides flour, corn and saw mills in good number and well distributed.

Athens, the capital town, situated on Oconee river, is the terminus of two railroads connecting it with all parts of the State, is market town for the county, has a population of 5,979—2,884 white, 3,095 black, 1,200 private dwellings, 2 hotels, 2 banks, 11 churches, 14 schools—including State University—with 700 scholars, 14 dry goods stores, 21 grocery stores, 2 drug stores, 2 weekly newspapers, 9 physicians, 15 lawyers, 4 dentists.

CLAYTON—Population, in 1870, 5,477—3,734 white, 1,743 black; about 1 per cent. of county too hilly, and a like per cent. too swampy, for cultivation; 75 per cent. of field laborers white; 19 public free schools for whites, 6 for blacks; Baptists have 12 churches, Methodists 10, Presbyterians 1, Lutherans 1; 10 flour and corn mills, 1 plough factory, 1 furniture factory, 1 carriage factory.

Jonesboro', the capital town, is on Central Railroad, 20 miles from Atlanta, the market town. (Details not reported.)

COLUMBIA—Population, in 1870, 13,529—4,080 white, 9,449 black; 1 per cent. of county too broken for tillage; 2½ per cent. irreclaimable swamp ; 70 per cent. of tillable land cleared; 80 per cent. of field laborers black ; 22 public free schools for whites, 1 for blacks; Baptist churches 10, Methodist 11; Georgia Railroad runs through southern portion of county, and Savannah river forms its northeastern boundary.

Appling, the capital town, is 10 miles from Savannah river, 9 miles from Georgia Railroad, 22 miles from Augusta, the market town; has a population of 114—38 whites, 76 blacks, 7 private dwellings, 1 hotel, 2 churches, 1 school with 25 scholars, 1 dry goods store, 1 grocery store, 1 physician, 1 lawyer.

COWETA—Population, in 1870, 15,875—7,856 white, 8,019 black ; 1 per cent. of land too broken for tillage; 48 per cent. of tillable land cleared; 69 per cent. of field laborers black : some gold discovered, but not mined to any considerable extent; 40 public free schools for whites, 26 for blacks; Baptist churches 12, Methodist 15; Presbyterian 4, Lutheran 1, Christian 2; 1 cotton factory, with 50 operatives ; 1 shoe factory ; 1 furniture factory, with 5 operatives ; 1 foundry, with 20 operatives.

Newnan, the capital town, is located at the crossing of the Atlanta & West Point and Savannah, Griffin & North Alabama Railroads, 40 miles from Atlanta, has a population of 2,000—1,200 white, 800 black, 350 private dwellings, 2 hotels, 2 banks, 6 churches, 7 schools with 310 scholars, 2 weekly newspapers, 15 dry goods and mixed stores, 13 grocery stores, 2 drug stores, 9 physicians, 11 lawyers, 2 dentists.

DEKALB—Population, in 1870, 10,014—7,352 white, 2,662 black. Except Stone Mountain and its rocky extensions—about 2,000 acres—the whole county is tillable, and 25 per cent. cleared ; gold exists to a limited extent, but is not mined ; 75 per cent. of farm laborers white ; 39 public free schools for whites, 14 for blacks; Methodists, Baptists, Presbyterians, the prevailing religious denominations; 2 cotton factories propelled by water, with 120 operatives ; several wagon factories, and ample supply of lumber, flour and corn mills.

Decatur, the capital town, eligibly situated on Georgia Railroad, 7 miles from Atlanta, and once a favorite resort in summer months, has 700 inhabitants—400 white, 300 black ; 80 private dwellings, 1 hotel, 5 churches, 2 schools with 100 pupils, 6 dry goods stores, 4 grocery stores, 4 physicians, 4 lawyers.

Stone Mountain, situated at the base of the wonderful natural curiosity of that name, and immediately on the Georgia Railroad, 16 miles from Atlanta, has a population of 1,150—900 white, 250 black, 140 private dwellings, 1 hotel, 4 churches, 1 weekly newspaper, 3 schools with 180 scholars, 14 stores of mixed merchandize, 6 physicians, 1 lawyer.

Douglas—Organized since last decennial census. (October 1870) out of parts of Campbell and Carroll; population not yet ascertained, but large proportion white; 10 per cent. of county too broken for tillage; 38 per cent. of tillable land cleared; 60 per cent. of field laborers white; no minerals now mined—gold formerly paid well; magnetic iron ore, copper, and asbestus exist, but not worked for want of capital; 14 public free schools for whites 3 for blacks; 9 Baptist churches, 9 Methodist, 1 Christian, 1 Unitarian, 1 Lutheran.

Douglasville, the capital town, is 18 miles from an operating railroad, but on one in process of construction, 25 miles from the market town, has 850 inhabitants—800 white, 50 black, 160 private dwellings, 1 hotel, 2 churches, 2 schools with 60 scholars, 6 dry goods stores, 7 grocery stores, 2 physicians, 5 lawyers, 1 dentist.

Elbert—Population, in 1870, 9,249—4,386 white, 4,863 black; nearly entire county tillable; 65 per cent. cleared, gold, black lead, iron ore have been discovered, but neither mined; 64 per cent. of farm laborers black; about 65 public free schools, very near equally divided between whites and blacks; 12 Baptist churches, 11 Methodist, 1 Presbyterian; flour, corn and lumber mills and tanyards the only manufacturing establishments.

Elberton, the capital town, is 13 miles from Savannah river, 40 miles from Athens, 75 from Augusta, 100 from Atlanta, 50 from Toccoa, with which latter place a railroad connection will be formed during the present year—1878; it has 600 inhabitants—375 white, 225 black; 74 private dwellings, 1 hotel, 4 churches, 4 schools with 120 pupils. 1 weekly newspaper, 7 dry goods stores, 8 grocery stores, 1 drug store, 3 physicians, 11 lawyers, 1 dentist.

Fayette—Population, in 1870, 8,221—5,683 white, 2,538 black; all the lands of the county believed to be tillable, and 50 per cent of them cleared; 60 per cent. of farm laborers white; 21 public free schools for whites, 11 for blacks; Baptists have 10 churches, Methodists 10, Christians 1.

Fayetteville, the capital town, is 9 miles from Jonesboro' on Central Railroad, 29 miles from Atlanta, the market town, has 130 inhabitants—100 white, 30 black, 25 private dwellings, 1 hotel, 2 churches, 1 school with 30 scholars, 2 mixed stores, 2 physicians, 4 lawyers.

Fulton—Population, in 1870, 33,446—18,164 white, 15,282 black, about 2½ per cent. of land too broken for tillage; 65 per cent. of tillable land cleared; 55 per cent. of farm laborers white; gold. serpentine, asbestus, iron pyrite, with some copper, gneiss and soapstone, are the principal minerals; there are 22 public free schools for whites, 8 for blacks, besides many private high schools; 12 Baptist churches, 14 Methodist, 5 Presbyterian, 4 Episcopal, 1 Congregational, 1 Christian, 1 Catholic, 1 Lutheran, 1 Hebrew;

1 cotton factory, 4 planing mills, 3] railroad car shops, 1 rolling mill, 6 iron foundries, 2 door and sash factories, 6 merchant flour mills, 2 soap factories, 1 large brewery, 2 paper mills, 2 ice factories, 1 boot and shoe factory, 3 candy factories, 2 paper box and bag factories, 2 cracker factories, 2 cotton-gin factories, 1 manufactory of agricultural implements.

Atlanta, the capital town, and seat of government of the State, may be said to be the railroad center of the South. It has an altitude of 1,087 feet above the sea, and is located on the water shed which divides the waters of the Atlantic from those of the Gulf of Mexico, in latitude 33°45'19.8", longitude 84°23'29.7". Population, in 1877, 35,956, (now considerably increased) about one-third black; has 8 hotels, 44 churches, 1 medical college with 100 students, 9 public free schools with 4,100 enrolled scholars—2,500 white, 1,600 black—56 teachers; private schools 5, pupils 350; Atlanta University, (colored) 125 students; Theological Seminary, (colored) 50 students; 1 daily paper, 8 weekly, 2 monthly, 2 periodicals, (monthly) 15 printing offices, 3 binderies, 9 banks, 50 dry goods stores, 9 shoe stores, 490 grocery stores, 36 drug stores, 27 fruit stores, 60 licensed physicians, 71 licensed lawyers, 8 dentists, 40 places of miscellaneous business.

GREENE—Population, in 1870, 12,454—4,298 white, 8,156 black; the entire county believed to be susceptible of tillage; 58 per cent. of it cleared; 90 per cent of field laborers black; 30 free public schools for whites, 20 for blacks; Baptists have 12 churches, Methodists 9, Presbyterians 4, Roman Catholics 1; about same number of Baptist and Methodist churches for blacks; several cotton factories, all now suspended; wagon and carriage factories, flour, corn and lumber mills abundant—also tanyards.

Greensboro', the capital town, is situated on Georgia Railroad, 87 miles from Augusta, the market town, has 1,200 inhabitants—600 white, 600 black, 70 private dwellings, 3 hotels, 4 churches, 2 schools with 50 pupils, 2 weekly newspapers, 6 dry goods stores, 2 grocery stores, 2 drug stores, 4 physicians, 11 lawyers, 1 dentist.

Union Point is a thriving village situated at the junction of the Georgia Railroad and the Athens branch of the same road; it is 39 miles by rail from Athens, 78 miles from Augusta and 93 from Atlanta; population 525 —whites 275, blacks 250; 4 churches, 2 schools, 6 stores, 3 lawyers, 3 physicians, 1 hotel.

HANCOCK—Population, in 1870, 11,317—3,645 white, 7,672 black; 56 per cent. of tillable land cleared; 80 per cent. of farm laborers black; 34 free public schools for whites, 15 for blacks; Baptist churches 9, Methodist 13, Presbyterian 2, Episcopal 1, Roman Catholic 1; 1 cotton mill, but now suspended; 1 sash and blind factory; several cotton-gin and carriage factories.

Sparta, the capital town, is situated on the Macon & Augusta Railroad, 50 miles from Macon and 70 from Augusta, the market town, though much cotton sold at the place; white population 570, black 250, private dwellings 70, hotels 2, banks 1, churches 4, schools 2, pupils 80, 1 weekly newspaper, 13 dry goods stores, 5 grocery stores, 2 drug stores, 7 physicians, 10 lawyers, 2 dentists.

HARRIS—Population, in 1870, 13,284—5,791 white, 7,493 black; 7 per cent. of county too mountainous for successful tillage; 75 per cent. of tillable land cleared; 66 per cent. of farm laborers black; 47 public free schools for whites, 23 for blacks; Baptists have 11 churches, Primitive Baptists 3, Methodists 13, Presbyterians 1; 2 cotton factories in the county, one employing about 250 hands, the other not in operation; flour, corn and saw mills abundant, and all necessary workshops.

Hamilton, the capital town is romantically situated in a valley between Pine and Oak mountains—peaks of a detached chain running through Upson, Talbot and Harris, to the Chattahoochee river. It is within two miles of the present terminus of the North & South Railroad, 22 miles from Columbus, the market town, 20 from West Point, 22½ from LaGrange; has 1,000 inhabitants—700 white, 300 black, 75 private dwellings, 2 hotels, 4 churches, 1 female college with 4 professors and 75 students, 2private schools, 1 weekly newspaper, 4 mixed stores, 2 grocery and liquor stores, 1 drug store, 3 physicians, 7 lawyers, 1 dentist.

HEARD—Population, in 1870, 7,866—5,218 white, 2,648 black; about 2 per cent. of county too broken for tillage; same amount of irreclaimable swamp; 50 per cent. of tillable land cleared; 62 per cent. of farm laborers white; gold, copper, iron and mica exist, but in small quantities; 32 public free schools for whites, 8 for blacks; Baptists churches 23, Methodist 17.

Franklin, the capital town, is 15 miles from a railroad, 20 miles from La-Grange, the market town of the county; has 300 inhabitants—250 white. 50 black, 30 private dwellings, 3 churches, 1 hotel, 1 school with 40 pupils, 11 mixed stores, 3 physicians, 4 lawyers, 2 dentists.

HENRY—Population, in 1870, 10,102—6,269 white, 3,833 black; about 1⅔ per cent. of county too broken for tillage; 3 per cent. too swampy; of tillable land 68 per cent. cleared; 50 per cent. of farm laborers white; some gold and iron, not sufficient for mining; public free schools for whites 35, for blacks 26; Baptist churches 15, Methodist 10, Presbyterian 1, Bible Christian 1; several wool-carding machines in county; also, wagon, carriage and furniture factories.

McDonough, the capital town, is ten miles from the Central Railroad and market town, 50 miles from Macon; has 400 inhabitants—275 white, 125 black; 46 private dwellings, 1 hotel, 3 churches, 1 school with 18 pupils, 4 dry-goods stores, 3 grocery stores, 1 drug store, 3 physicians, 3 lawyers.

JASPER.—Population in 1870, 10,439—3,884 white, 6,555 black; about 3½ per cent. of county too broken for profitable tillage, and 1⅔ per cent. too swampy; of tillable land 40 per cent. is cleared, 67 per cent. of farm laborers black; 23 public free schools for whites, 14 for blacks; Baptist churches 12, Methodist 10; Presbyterian 1; abundant water powers but no manufactures except flour, corn and lumber mills.

Monticello, the capital town, is 20 miles from the Georgia Railroad, and Madison the market town, (details not reported.)

JONES.—Population in 1870, 9,436—2,991 white, 6,445 black; about two per cent. of county too hilly for tillage, 1 per cent. irreclaimable swamp, 62 per cent. of tillable land cleared, 84 per cent. of farm laborers black; 13

public free schools for whites, 19 for blacks; Baptist churches 8, Methodist 9; flour, corn and lumber mills abundant.

Clinton, the capital town, is 6 miles from Macon and Augusta Railroad, 12 miles from Macon, the market town; has a population of 250—100 white, 150 black, 32 private dwellings, 1 hotel, 2 churches, 2 schools with 70 scholars, 2 dry-goods stores, 2 grocery stores, 4 physicians, 4 lawyers.

LINCOLN.—Population in 1870, 5,413—1,797 white, 3,616 black; about 2½ per cent. of county too broken for tillage, 37 per cent. of tillable land cleared, 64 per cent of farm laborers black; gold, silver, copper, lead, rutile, manganese and several precious stones exist; gold mined extensively by several companies with handsome profits, the mines paying as well as any in State; with capital, gold is destined to become an immense interest; Norman mine, near Goshen, has yielded very handsomely in last 4 months. County has 11 public free schools for whites, 8 for blacks; Baptist churches 6, Methodist 8, Presbyterian 1; flour, corn and lumber mills, small wood and iron shops the only manufacturing interests.

Lincolnton, the capital town, is 7 miles from Savannah river, 18 miles from Washington, 20 miles from Thomson, on Georgia Railroad, and 45 miles from Augusta, the principal market town; has 146 inhabitants—106 white, 40 black; 16 private dwellings, 1 hotel, 2 churches, 1 school with 30 scholars, 2 dry-goods stores, 2 grocery stores, 2 physicians, 2 lawyers.

McDUFFIE.—Having been formed in 1871 out of parts of Warren and Columbia, and since the date of the last census, population not ascertained; 50 per cent. of tillable land cleared; 68 per cent. of farm laborers black; gold found in large deposits and veins in northern part of county and worked successfully for many years, mines still in operation and paying handsomely; copper exists in same section, but is not mined; there are 19 public free schools for whites, 8 for blacks; only religious denominations Baptist and Methodist, former has 5 churches, latter 6, besides churches for blacks; wagons, buggies, flour, lumber, leather, only articles manufactured in county.

Thomson, the capital town is on Georgia Railroad, 30 miles from Augusta, same distance from Savannah river; (details not reported.)

MERIWETHER.—Population in 1870, 13,756—6,387 white, 7,369 black; 6 per cent. of lands too mountainous or broken for successful tillage, 78½ per cent. of tillable land cleared, 80 per cent of farm laborers black; gold mines in northwestern portion of county been worked on considerable scale and with good success for many years, there are 44 public free schools for whites, 15 for blacks; religious denominations, Methodist and Baptist chiefly and about equal in number; some Presbyterians; county noted for its mineral spring.

Greenville, the capital town, is 15 miles from the Atlanta and West Point Railroad, 20 miles from LaGrange, 45 miles from Columbus, both being market towns; (details not reported).

MONROE.—Population in 1870, 17,213—6,409 white, 10,804 black, entire county considered susceptible of cultivation, 85 per cent. of original forest cleared; 80 per cent. of farm laborers black; copper believed to exist, but no mining; 31 public free schools for whites, 23 for blacks; has 10 Baptist churches, 15 Methodist, 1 Presbyterian, 5 or 6 large merchant mills, with many smaller mills.

Forsyth, the capital town, is situated on the Central Railroad, 26 miles north of Macon, 77 from Atlanta, 12 from Ocmulgee river; has 2,300 inhabitants—1,200 white, 1,100 black, 225 private dwellings, two hotels, 1 bank, 5 churches, 5 schools including a female college with an aggregate of 250 scholars, 1 weekly newspaper, 12 dry-goods stores, 9 grocery stores, 3 drug stores, 3 physicians, 11 lawyers, 4 dentists.

Morgan.—Population in 1870, 10,696—3,637 white, 7,058 black; about 5 per cent. of county too broken or hilly for profitable cultivation, 2 per cent. irreclaimable swamp, 62½ per cent. of original forest cleared, 76 per cent. of farm laborers black, gold mined to a small extent twenty-five years ago; a bed of mica recently discovered; county has 34 public free schools for whites, 17 for blacks; religious denominations, Baptist 9 churches, Methodist 10, Presbyterian 1, Episcopal 1, Primitive Baptist 2; 1 cotton factory with 300 operatives, carriage and wagon factories, flour, corn and lumber mills ample for public wants.

Madison, the capital town, is on the Georgia Railroad 68 miles from Atlanta, 103 from Augusta, and is the market town for the inhabitants generally, has a population of 2,700—1,400 white, 1,300 black, 171 private dwellings, 2 banks, 6 churches, 2 hotels, 5 schools with 95 scholars, 1 weekly newspaper, 15 dry-goods stores, 17 grocery stores, 2 drug stores, 1 hardware store, 5 physicians, 11 lawyers, 2 dentists.

Newton.—Population in 1870, 14,615—8,601 white, 6,014 black; 63 per cent. of tillable land cleared, 55 per cent. of farm laborers black; gold found but never mined successfully; 1 male college, 1 female college, 33 public free schools for whites, 16 for blacks; Baptists have 12 churches, Methodists 12, Presbyterians 3; 2 cotton mills now confined to yarns, 1 woolen mill, flour, corn and lumber mills abundant.

Covington, the capital town and market for county, is on Georgia Railroad 41 miles from Atlanta, 130 from Augusta, has 1,250 inhabitants—600 white, 650 black, 250 dwellings, 2 hotels, 1 bank, 5 churches, 1 female college, and 2 schools for whites, aggregating 200 scholars, 2 schools for blacks, 2 weekly newspapers, 14 dry-goods stores, 7 grocery stores, 1 furniture store, 1 book store, 1 drug store, 5 physicians, 2 lawyers, 3 dentists.

Oxford, seat of Emory College, on Georgia Railroad, 1 mile from Covington, has 1,050 inhabitants—800 white, 250 black, 75 private dwellings, 3 churches, 4 schools with 250 scholars, 2 grocery stores, 2 physicians, 2 lawyers.

Oconee.—County organized February, 1875, from a portion of Clarke, and census not ascertained; of tillable land 58 per cent. cleared, 57 per cent. of farm hands black; has 19 public free schools for whites, 7 for blacks, 8 Baptist Churches, 7 Methodist, 4 Christian; 3 cotton factories on the county line, manufactories of carriages, wagons, leather, shoes.

Watkinsville, the capital town, is 7 miles from Athens, the market town, same distance from a railroad, has 344 inhabitants—194 white, 150 black, 34 private dwellings, 1 hotel, 1 church, 2 schools with 85 scholars, 3 dry-goods stores, 1 grocery store, 2 physicians, 3 lawyers, 1 dentist.

Oglethorpe.—Population in 1870, 11,782—4,641 white, 7,141 black; 3 per cent. of county too broken for successful cultivation, 50 per cent. of tillable land cleared, 70 per cent. of farm laborers black ; gold and copper exist, a belt of former running through county northeast and southwest, very rich at points and with capital to work it would pay well ; has 29 public free schools for whites, 9 for blacks; 2 Baptist churches ; 15 Methodist, 2 Presbyterian ; no manufactories except the usual mills and shops.

Lexington, the capital town, is 3 miles from Athens branch Georgia Railroad, 16 miles from Athens, the market town of the county, has a population of 600—225 whites, 375 blacks, 65 private residences, 3 churches, 3 schools with 90 scholars, 1 weekly newspaper, 3 dry-goods stores, 3 grocery stores, 3 physicians, 5 lawyers, 1 dentist.

Pike.—Population in 1870, 10,905—5,999 white, 4,906 black; about 2 per cent. of county too broken and same amount too swampy for successful tillage ; of tillable land 70 per cent. cleared, 52 per cent of farm laborers white; 31 public free schools for whites, 15 for blacks'; 24 Baptist churches, 22 Methodist; 1 Presbyterian ; carriages, buggies, furniture only manufactures of county.

Zebulon, the capital town, is 9 miles from Central Railroad, 8 and 12 miles from the two market towns, 40 miles from Ocmulgee river ; has 250 inhabitants—150 white, 100 black, 28 private dwellings, 1 hotel, 2 churches, 1 school with 50 pupils, 2 dry-goods stores, 2 grocery stores, 3 physicians, 3 lawyers.

Barnesville, on Central Railroad, 61 miles from Atlanta, 42 from Macon, has 2,100 inhabitants—1,500 white, 1,100 black, 400 private dwellings, 1 hotel, 1 bank, 4 churches, 4 schools including 1 institute, 350 pupils, 1 weekly newspaper, 10 dry-goods stores, 12 grocery stores, 3 drug stores, 4 physicians, 7 lawyers, 1 dentist.

Milner, on Central Railroad, 54 miles from Atlanta, 49 miles from Macon, has 550 inhabitants—350 white, 200 black; 75 private dwellings, 1 hotel, 2 churches, 1 school with 65 scholars, 9 dry-goods stores, 3 grocery stores, 2 lawyers, 3 physicians.

Putnam.—Population in 1870, 10,461—3,016 white, 7,445 black ; ½ of 1 per cent. of lands too broken for successful tillage, 2½ per cent. too swampy, 50 per cent of tillable land cleared, 82 per cent of farm laborers black ; iron pyrite, only mineral of value known to exist; about 40 public free schools with private high school at county site; 12 Baptist churches, 18 Methodist, 1 Presbyterian ; leather, shoes, flour and lumber principal manufactures ; two cotton factories destroyed during the war never rebuilt, sites among the best in the State.

Eatonton, the capital town and market of the county, is terminus of Eatonton branch Central Railroad, 40 miles from Gordon, 50 miles from Macon via railroad : 1,601 inhabitants—600 white, 1,001 black—100 private dwellings, 1 hotel, 4 churches, 5 schools including high school with 175 pupils, 1 weekly newspaper, 10 dry-goods stores ; 6 grocery stores, 1 drug store, 4 physician, 7 lawyers, 2 dentists.

Rockdale.—Laid off October, 1870, out of parts of Newton and Henry and census not ascertained ; 4½ per cent of lands too rocky for cultivation, 68 per cent. of tillable land cleared, 63 per cent. of farm laborers white ; 21 public free schools for whites, 11 for blacks ; Baptist churches 10, Methodist

10; Presbyterian 2; 1 large paper mill 30 operatives, 1 cotton factory, buggy and chair factories, flour and lumber mills.

Conyers, the capital town and market for the county, is on Georgia Railroad 31 miles from Atlanta and 140 from Augusta, (details not reported).

SPALDING.—Population in 1870, 10,205—5,327 white, 4,878 black ; 2½ per cent. of lands too broken for successful tillage, 3 per cent, too swampy, 63 per cent. of tillable land cleared, 57 per cent. of farm laborers ᵕlack ; no minerals ; 22 public free schools for whites, 14 for blacks, besides private schools ; 16 Baptist churches, 15 Methodist, 2 Presbyterian, 1 Episcopal, 3 Christian, 1 Lutheran ; carriages, wagons, furniture, leather, flour and lumber comprise the manufactures of county.

Griffin, the capital town, is on the Central Railroad, 41 miles from Atlanta, 62 miles from Macon, is market town of county ; has 2 banks, (details not reported.)

TALBOT.—Population in 1870, 11,913—4,761 white, 7,152 black ; 6 per cent. of lands too mountainous for tillage, 2¾ per cent. irreclaimable swamp, 71½ per cent. of tillable land cleared ; iron ore exists ; public free schools ample for all purposes ; Baptist churches 11, Methodist 14, Presbyterian 2, Episcopal 1 ; 1 gin factory, carriage factories, tanneries, flour and lumber mills, and 1 rice mill.

Talbotton, the capital town, is 7 miles from the Southwestern Railroad, 30 miles from Columbus, the market town, and from a navigable stream ; has 1,000 inhabitants—600 white, 400 black, 150 private dwellings, 1 hotel, 5 churches, 4 schools with 150 scholars, 2 weekly newspapers, 1 steam flour and corn mill, 4 dry-goods stores, 7 grocery stores, 1 hardware store, 2 drug stores, 3 physicians, 10 lawyers, 2 dentists.

Geneva, on the Southwestern Railroad, 30 miles from Columbus, has 250 inhabitants—175 white, 75 black; 25 private dwellings, 1 hotel, 2 churches, 2 schools with 60 pupils, 6 dry-goods stores, 5 grocery stores, 1 physician, 2 lawyers.

TALIAFERRO.—Population in 1870, 4,796—1,809 white, 2,987 black ; entire area of county considered tillable, 50 per cent. of land cleared ; 70 per cent. of farm laborers white; 21 free public schools for whites, 9 for blacks ; 8 Baptist churches, 2 Methodist, 1 Presbyterian, 1 Roman Catholic ; furniture, carriages, wagons, flour, lumber only manufactures.

Crawfordville, the capital town, is on the Georgia Railroad, 64 miles from Augusta, 107 from Atlanta, has a population of 500—300 white, 200 black ; 50 private dwellings, 1 hotel, 3 churches, 1 weekly newspaper, 10 mixed stores, 1 drug store, 5 physicians, 8 lawyers, 1 dentist.

TROUP.—Population in 1870, 17,632—6,408 white, 11,224 black : 3½ per cent. of land too broken for tillage, 5 per cent. irreclaimable swamp, 77 per cent. of tillable land cleared ; mica and asbestus exist in large beds ; 41 public free schools for whites, 32 for blacks ; Baptist churches 13, Methodist 13, Presbyterian 4 ; Troup cotton factory has 100 hands, Chattahoochee cotton factory on State line 100 hands.

LaGrange, the capital town, situated on Atlanta and West-Point Railroad, 70 miles from Atlanta, 44 miles from Columbus, is market town of the county, has 2,250 inhabitants—875 white, 1,375 black; 475 private dwellings,

2 hotels, 5 churches, 6 schools with 702 pupils, 1 weekly newspaper, 9 dry-goods stores, 20 grocery stores and confectionaries, 2 drug stores, 5 physicians, 18 lawyers, 3 dentists.

West Point is situated on the Chattahoochee River, is the terminus of the Atlanta and West Point Railroad, 87 miles from Atlanta, 17 miles from LaGrange, has 2,310 inhabitants—1,370 white, 940 black; 207 private dwellings, 3 hotels, 2 banks, 5 churches, 2 schools with 300 pupils, 2 weekly newspapers, 10 dry-goods stores, 2 shoe stores, 18 grocery stores, 3 drug stores, 1 hardware store, 3 warehouses, 7 physicians, 5 lawyers, 1 dentist.

UPSON.—Population in 1870, 9,430—4,865 white, 4,565 black; 2 per cent. of county too broken for cultivation, of tillable land 50 per cent. cleared ; minerals—gold, iron, the best of granite and sand stone for building; water-powers unsurpassed; 57 per cent. of farm laborers white ; 27 public free schools for whites, 7 for blacks; Baptist churches 12, Methodist 14, Presbyterian 1, besides negro churches ; 3 cotton factories, 1 wood machine works, flour and lumber mills abundant.

Thomaston, the capital town, is the terminus of Thomaston branch of Central Railroad, 17 miles from Barnesville, 78 miles from Atlanta, 60 from Macon ; is the market town of county, has 900 inhabitants—650 white, 250 black; 125 private dwellings, 1 hotel, 4 churches, 2 schools with 150 pupils, 1 weekly newspaper, 9 dry goods stores, 7 grocery stores, 5 physicians, 7 lawyers, 1 dentist.

WALTON.—Population in 1870, 11,038—6,876 white, 4,162 black; 1½ per cent. of county too broken for tillage, 13 irreclaimable swamp; of tillable land 63 per cent. cleared; 53 per cent. of farm laborers black; 39 public free schools for whites, 10 for blacks ; Baptists have 14 churches, Methodists 9, Presbyterians 1; negro churches 8—all Baptist and Methodist; 1 cotton factory, 1 woollen mill, numerous flour and lumber mills.

Monroe, the capital town, is 10 miles from Social Circle, 22 miles from Madison, 24 from Athens ; has 1,000 inhabitants—700 white, 300 black ; 125 private dwellings, 2 hotels, 4 churches, three schools. with 150 pupils, 6 dry goods stores, 6 grocery stores, 1 drug store, 4 physicians, 6 lawyers.

Social Circle, on Georgia Railroad, the market town of the county, 52 miles from Atlanta, 119 from Augusta, has a population of whites 550, blacks 320—total, 870 ; 18 private dwellings, 2 hotels 2, churches. 1 school with 65 scholars, 1 weekly newspaper, 7 dry goods stores, 2 drug stores, 5 physicians, 2 lawyers and 2 dentists.

WARREN.—Population in 1870, 10,545—4,285 white, 6,260 black ; whole area considered tillable, 25 per cent. cleared and in cultivation. 66 per cent. of farm laborers black ; gold formerly mined with profit, but no mining at present ; 26 public free schools for whites, 10 for blacks; Baptist churches 18, Methodist 20; Rock Mills Cotton Factory employs 175 hands, flour and lumber mills ample.

Warrenton, the capital town, is on Macon and Augusta Railroad, 50 miles from Augusta, the market town, by rail, 75 miles from Macon. (details not reported).

WILKES.—Population in 1870, 11,796—3,969 white, 7,827 black ; ½ of one per cent. too broken for successful tillage, 1 per cent. irreclaimable swamp,

63½ per cent. in cultivation, 16½ per cent. in original forest, 20 per cent. pine old fields, 78 per cent. of farm laborers white; gold, lead, copper, and iron ores exist, but none mined except gold, to a limited extent; one mine in southeastern portion of county being worked with handsome profit. There are 22 public free schools for whites, 10 for blacks, besides private schools; 14 Baptist churches, 8 Methodist, 1 Episcopal, 1 Presbyterian, 1 Roman Catholic; carriages, wagons, leather, flour, lumber, and usual wood and iron work, the only manufactures of county.

Washington, the capital town. is the northern terminus of Washington branch Georgia Railroad, 18 miles from the main line, 75 from Augusta by rail, 52 by wagon road, 20 miles from pole-boat navigation on Savannah river; it has 1,800 inhabitants—600 white, 1, 200 black, 100 residences for whites, 2 hotels, 1 bank. 3 schools with 130 pupils, 1 weekly newspaper, 11 dry goods stores, 6 grocery stores. 2 drug stores, 4 physicians, 10 lawyers, 1 dentist. This is the first place in the United States named in honor of the Father of his country.

EAST GEORGIA.

This division of the State embraces the country lying between the heads of tide water in the east, and the Ocmulgee River in the west, and south to the corner of Liberty, Tattnall, and Appling, while the counties of Twiggs, Wilkinson, Washington, Glascock, Jefferson and Richmond. indicate its limits in the North. It differs from Middle Georgia in several important respects; its geological formations are tertiary instead of metamorphic; its average elevation is only about 250 feet above the sea; its surface is more level; its soils, for the most part, loamy or sandy; subsoil clay, red and yellow, 4 to 6 inches below the surface in clay lands, 8 to 12 inches in sandy lands; its forest growth is principally pine; it contains calcareous marls in considable deposits. It is also the commencement of the section in which the sugar cane can be profitably cultivated, while its rocks, which are few, are of a sedimentary character, with iron ore and Buhr stone in several localities. Deposits of kaolin and pipe clay are found along its entire length from east to west. Its water powers are less than those of Middle Georgia, and its drinking water, while good, is less cool and pure. While pine is the leading forest growth, and the chief timber for building and export; there are also large bodies of oak and hickory. The soils in such localities are either clayey or gray, mostly the latter, and admirably adapted to the production of cotton and corn; cypress abounds in the swamps and lowlands. The county of Burke was, for many years, and until the late revolution in our system of labor, the leading cotton producing county of the State The comparatively fresh lands of Decatur have, of late years, enabled her to claim and hold the championship in this particular product. Cotton, with corn, wheat, (the adaptation to which lessens as we proceed southward into the pine lands,) oats, rye, barley, sugar cane, potatoes, constitute the staple products of the section. The average yields per acre with fair culture: are cotton, 650 lbs.; corn, 14 bushels; wheat, 12 bushels; oats, 25 bushels; cane syrup, 300 gallons; potatoes, 150 bushels; barley 30 bushels. There is much high culture in the district, and these results are often quadrupled. The seasons for planting and harvesting are nearly the same as those of Middle Georgia, perhaps from 10 to 14 days earlier. The district is famous for its excellent fruit, especially peaches, strawberries and melons, large quantities of which are exported annually to northern markets. Richmond, Burke and Washington being the principal counties engaged in the trade. The fig, grape—especially scuppernong—pear, plum, are all grown successfully. All the vegetables thrive well.

The district is well watered, and water powers are ample for all purposes. The climate is perceptibly milder in winter than that of Middle Georgia, and the average temperature in summer higher; snows light, and only fall once in every four or five years. The average price of wood-land in the oak and hickory section is $7 to $10 per acre, and improved lands $4 to $6; in the pine country uncleared lands can be bought from $1 to $2 per acre; improved farms from $3 to $4. Both can be had on a liberal credit. In the upper half of the district, the average wages of good field hands is $9 per month, with rations; in the pine lands, $7; ordinary mechanics, $1 to $2 per day.

The people are among the best in the State, and desire to fill up their surplus lands with industrious and thrifty immigrants.

The Bermuda and sedge grasses of the old fields in the upper tier of counties, and the wire grass and cane of the southern tier, afford the finest ranges for cattle and sheep the greater portion of the year. The southern counties abound in fish, deer, and nearly every species of wild game.

COUNTIES.

BULLOCH.—Population, in 1870, 5,610—3,866 white, 1,744 black; county has 6 per cent. irreclaimable swamp, 21 per cent of tillable land cleared, prevailing forest growth pine and cypress, with some oak, hickory, magnolia, elm; has 47 public free schools for whites, 5 for blacks: 15 Baptist churches, 5 Methodist, 1 Presbyterian, 1 Roman Catholic; 64 per cent. of farm laborers white.

Statesboro, the capital town, is 10 miles from Central Railroad, 40 miles from Savannah River, 55 miles from Savannah, the market town; (details not reported).

BURKE—Population in 1870, 17,679—3,866 white, 13,436 black; 5 per cent. of county irreclaimable swamp, 62 per cent. of tillable land cleared; 76 per cent. of farm laborers black; iron ore in abundance and worked with profit during the late war; Buhr stone of excellent quality, quarried to a limited extent, marl in large and valuable deposits; 20 public free schools for whites, 13 for blacks; Baptist churches 13, Methodist 12, Presbyterian 2, all for whites; negroes have about same number; no manufacturing except flour and lumber; county regarded as one of the richest and most prosperous in the State.

Waynesboro, the capital town, is on the Waynesboro branch of the Central Railroad, 30 miles from Augusta, the market town, 100 miles from Savannah, 20 miles from Savannah river; has 800 inhabitants—400 white, 400 black, 51 private residences, 1 hotel, 4 churches, 3 schools with 175 pupils, 1 weekly newspaper, 11 stores of mixed merchandise, 2 drug stores, 2 physicians, 11 lawyers, 1 dentist.

DODGE.—Having been laid off from parts of Telfair, Pulaski, and Montgomery, in 1870, population not given in census of that year; 5 per cent. of county too swampy for cultivation, 15 per cent. of tillable land cleared; 95 per cent. of forest growth yellow pine, same per cent. of soil sandy or sandy loam; 50 per cent. of farm laborers white; has 15 public free schools for whites, 3 for blacks, besides private schools; 12 Baptist churches, 10 Methodist, 1 Presbyterian; naval stores and lumber leading manufactures, sawmills and turpentine distilleries numerous, 3 shingle factories.

Eastman, the capital town, on Macon and Brunswick Railroad, 56 miles from Macon, 130 miles from Brunswick, 12 miles from Ocmulgee river; has a population of 500—300 white, 200 black; 1 splendid hotel—a favorite winter resort for northern invalids, 30 private residences, some very elegant; no churches, 1 high school with 40 scholars, 1 weekly newspaper, 5 dry-goods stores, 4 grocery stores, 3 physicians, 6 lawyers.

EMANUEL.—Population in 1870, 6,134—4,431 white, 1,703 black; has 4 per cent. irreclaimable swamp, 11 per cent. of tillable land cleared, 82 per cent. of farm laborers white; 33 public free schools for whites, 6 for blacks; 22 Baptist churches, 8 Methodist; 3 steam and 2 water lumber mills, 3 distilleries of turpentine, 2 carriage factories.

Swainsboro, the capital town, is 17 miles from Central Railroad, is the terminus of a projected branch road; is 4 miles from Ohoopee river, 80 miles from Savannah, the market town of county; has 420 inhabitants—400 white, 20 black; 25 private dwellings, 1 hotel, 2 churches, 1 school with 40 scholars, 1 weekly newspaper, 3 dry-goods stores, 3 grocery stores, 3 physicians, 4 lawyers.

GLASCOCK.—Population in 1870,· 2,736—1,917 white, 819 black; about 1 per cent. of county irreclaimable swamp, 20 per cent. of tillable land cleared; about 20 per cent. of soil clay, rest sandy; 66 per cent. of farm laborers white; 12 public free schools for whites, 4 for blacks; 6 Baptist and 7 Methodist churches.

Gibson, the capital town, is 14 miles from Augusta and Macon Railroad, 15 miles from Central Railroad, 40 miles from Augusta, the market town, (details not reported).

JEFFERSON.—Population, in 1870, 12,190—4,247 white, 7,943 black; 6 per cent. of the county too swampy for cultivation, 70 per cent. of lands sandy, same proportion originally pine forest; of tillable land, 59 per cent. cleared; 74 per cent. of farm laborers black; a a quarry of superior Buhr stone in south-eastern corner has been worked with profit, no other minerals reported; there are 32 public free schools for whites, 8 for blacks; Baptist churches 10, Methodist 11, Presbyterian 3, Roman Catholic, 1; flour and lumber mills the only manufactures of county.

Louisville, the capital town, and for many years the capital of the State, is 10 miles from the Central Railroad, 45 miles from Augusta. 110 miles from Savannah, the market town of the county; has 550 inhabitants—300 white, 250 black; 75 private dwellings, 2 hotels, 4 churches, 4 schools with 70 pupils, 1 weekly newspaper, 6 dry goods stores, 4 grocery stores, 1 drug store, 5 physicians, 6 lawyers, 1 dentist.

JOHNSON.—Population, in 1870, 2,964—2,049 white, 915 black; forest growth chiefly pine, 16 per cent. clay lands, with oak and hickory growth, 5 per cent. irreclaimable swamp; about 20 per cent, of tillable land cleared; 80 per cent. of farm laborers white; several deposits of marl, but not utilized; 14 public free schools, all for whites; Baptist churches 6, Methodist 11; no manufacturing.

Wrightsvil'e, the capital town, is 15 miles from Central railroad, 120 from Savannah, principal market town, 80 miles from Augusta, 70 miles from Macon, (details not reported).

LAURENS.—Population, in 1870, 7,834—4,180 white, 3,654 black; 2½ per cent. of county irreclaimable swamp, 25 per cent. of tillable land cleared, 20 per cent. clay lands, 80 per cent. sandy and sandy loam; 58 per cent, of farm laborers black; prevailing forest growth yellow pine of best quality for lumber; 31 public free schools for whites, 8 for blacks; Baptist churches 18, Methodist 8; flour, lumber, wagons and leather the only manufactures of county.

Dublin, the capital town, is on the Oconee River, 25 miles from Central Railroad, 30 miles from Macon and Brunswick Railroad, 55 miles from Macon, 160 from Savannah; population 532—white 233, black 299; private dwellings—of whites 46, blacks 34; hotels 2, churches—for whites 1, for blacks 1; schools—for whites 1 with 46 pupils, for blacks 1 with 40 pupils; weekly newspapers 2, dry goods stores 7, grocery stores 3, drug stores 1, physicians 2, lawyers 5, steam grist mills 2, steam saw mills 1, steam gins 2.

MONTGOMERY.—Population in 1870, 3,576—2,488 white, 1,108 black; 2 per cent. of lands too broken for successful tillage, 4 per cent. irreclaimable swamps, 7 per cent. of tillable land cleared, forest growth chiefly long-leaf pine of best quality; with hickory, cypress, maple, poplar, in low land; some small deposits of marl, large ones of peat, neither utilized in farming; 72 per cent. of farm laborers white; 20 public free schools, all for whites; Baptist churches 10, Methodist 18, Presbyterian 2; wool-carding, flour, and lumber mills in good supply; lumber and turpentine staple products.

Mt. Vernon, the capital town, is situated on Oconee River, (navigable) 17 miles from Macon and Brunswick R. R., 100 miles from Savannah, the market town, though much produce sold at railroad stations; has 157 inhabitants—97 white, 60 black, 24 private dwellings, 2 hotels, 1 church building with two congregations, 1 school with 35 pupils, 3 dry-goods stores, 2 grocery stores, 1 drug store, 1 physican, 5 lawyers.

PULASKI.—Population in 1870, 11,940—5,955 white, 5,984 black; 4 per cent. of county irreclaimable swamp, 4 5 per cent. of tillable lands cleared, 73 per cent. of farm laborers black, some calcareous marls, but not utilized; 29 public free schools for whites, 15 for blacks; Baptist churches 20, Methodist 15, Episcopal 1, Presbyterian 1; 1 cotton factory, 3,000 spindles, 1 wool-carding machine, 5 carriage shops, flour and lumber mills, ordinary work shops in good number; ¾ of forest timber pine and of superior quality.

Hawkinsville, the capital town, is on the west bank of Ocmugee River and the terminus of a branch of Macon and Brunswick R. R., 53 miles from Macon by rail; is principal market town of county; has 1 bank, (details not reported.)

6

RICHMOND.—Population in 1871, 25,724—13,157 white, 12,567 black ; 5 per cent. of county irreclaimable swamp, 70 per cent. of tillable land already cleared ; 75 per cent. of forest growth long-leaf pine, rest oak, hickory, poplar, gum, walnut ; 65 per cent. of field laborers white ; kaolin in large quantities is shipped to northern cities ; public free schools, (country) have 45 teachers, average number of pupils 1,102 ; Baptist churches 18, Methodist 18, Episcopal 3, Presbyterian 4, Roman Catholic 2, Lutheran 1, Unitarian 1, Christian 1, Hebrew 1 ; 4 large cotton factories, 3 large merchant flour mills, 2 fertilizer manufactories.

Augusta, the capital town, is situated on the west bank of Savannah River, 250 miles by water from its mouth, and is the terminus of 5 railroads ; population, in 1877, 23,768—15,136 white, 8,632 black ; has 500 private dwellings, 4 hotels, 17 churches for whites, 12 for blacks ; 4 high schools with 7 teachers, 165 average number of pupils ; city common schools with 30 teachers, average number of pupils 1,353 ; private schools with 14 teachers and 300 pupils ; 6 banks, 2 daily newspapers, 1 weekly newspaper, 1 medical college, 31 dry goods stores, 188 grocery stores, 17 drug stores, 52 lawyers, 42 physicians, 9 dentists. Manufactories : Augusta Factory, manufactures sheeting, shirting and drilling ; has 24,000 spindles, 800 looms, annual production, 314,873 pieces, 14,777,337 yards, 4,646,108 pounds, capital $600,000 ; Enterprise Manufacturing Company, sheeting and drilling ; has 7,300 spindles (to be increased to 12,800), capital $150,000 ; Richmond Factory, osnaburgs, stripes, thread and woolen goods, 3,500 spindles, capital $60,000 ; Globe Cotton Mills, bats, yarn and warp, 1,500 spindles ; Augusta Canal Manufacturing Company, carpet yarn, twine, etc., 1,020 spindles. Three large merchant flour mills—Paragon, Excelsior, Forest—stones and capacity not ascertained ; Barry's Chemical Fertilizer Manufacturing Company, and Georgia Chemical Works, capital, etc., not ascertained.

SCREVEN—Population, in 1870, 9,175—4,287 white, 4,888 black ; 3½ per cent. of lands irreclaimable swamp, 12 per cent. of tillable land cleared ; 56 per cent. of farm laborers black ; 66 per cent. of soil sandy, same per cent. of forest growth pine ; of minerals—limestone abundant in north-west part of county and burned to considerable extent ; Buhr stone also quarried to some extent, calcareous marls exist in good supply and are accessible ; there are 29 public free schools for whites, 15 for blacks ; Baptists have 30 churches, Methodists 3, Christians 1 ; 2 turpentine distilleries with 100 operatives in each, several wagon, carriage and plough factories, flour and lumber mills ; cattle and wool are large interests.

Sylvania, the capital town, is 12 miles from Central Railroad, 12 miles from Savannah River, 60 miles by rail to Savannah, the market town ; has 300 inhabitants—200 white, 100 black ; 25 private dwellings, 1 hotel, 2 churches, 1 school with 35 pupils, 3 mixed stores, 1 physician, 6 lawyers.

TATNALL.—Population in 1870, 4,860—3,580 white, 1,280 black ; the entire area reported susceptible of cultivation, 4 per cent. of tillable land cleared, 87½ per cent. sandy pine land, 68 per cent. of farm laborers white, some calcareous marls ; large quanties of peat available for agricultural purposes ; 29 public free schools for whites, 7 for blacks ; Baptists have 11 churches, Methodists 14 ; timber and lumber chief manufactures, large trade in both ; sheep and stock range excellent and perennial.

Reidsville, the capital town, is 40 miles from Atlantic and Gulf Railroad, 32 from Macon and Brunswick Railroad, 12 miles from Altamaha River, 2 miles from Great Ohoopee, both navigable; has 85 white inhabitants, 12 private dwellings, 1 hotel, 1 bank, 1 school with 30 pupils, 2 dry goods stores, 2 grocery stores, 1 physician, 3 lawyers, 1 dentist.

TELFAIR.—Population in 1870, 3,245 ; 2,100 white, 1,145 black ; has 8 per cent. of irreclaimable swamp, 17 per cent. of tillable land cleared, 50 per cent. stiff pebbly soil, rest sandy ; 50 per cent. of farm laborers white; long leaf pine exclusive growth of uplands, timber of superior quality ; 17 public free schools for white , 3 for blacks ; Baptists have 6 churches, Methodists 10 ; 1 steam shingle and grist mill, 2 steam saw mills, 6 turpentine distilleries.

McRae, the capital town, on Macon and Brunswick Railroad, 8 miles from Macon, 130 from Savannah, the market town, 17½ miles from Ocmulgee river, has 350 inhabitants—200 white, 150 black ; 25 private dwellings, 1 church, 1 school with 30 pupils, 3 dry goods stores, 4 grocery stores, 1 lawyer, no physician.

TWIGGS.—Population in 1870, 8,545—2,913 white, 5,632 black ; 5 per cent. of area irreclaimable swamp, 80 per cent. of tillable land cleared, about 60 per cent. sandy pine land, 70 per cent. of farm laborers black ; 1ᵃ public free schools for whites, 10 for blacks ; Baptists have 6 churches, Methodists 9 ; flour and lumber only manufactures.

Jeffersonville, the capital town, is 12 miles from Central Railroad, 12 miles from Ocmulgee river, 23 miles from Macon, the market town ; (details not reported.)

WASHINGTON.—Population in 1870, 15,842—7,530 white, 8,312 black ; 3½ per cent. of area irreclaimable swamp, 52½ per cent. of tillable land cleared, 50 per cent. clay soil with oak and hickory growth, remainder sandy with pine forest ; 81 per cent. of field laborers black ; of minerals—opal (white, gray, yellow,) extensive beds of calcareous marl, kaolin, potter's clay, etc., etc. ; 46 public free schools for whites, 8 for blacks ; Baptists and Methodists have, each, about 20 churches, Roman Catholics 1, Bible Christians 4 ; 1 pottery, lumber and flour mills the only manufacturing interests.

Sandersville, the capital town, is the terminus of a short railroad connecting with Central Railroad at Tennille, 60 miles from Augusta, 65 miles from Macon, 135 miles from Savannah, the market town, 14 miles from Oconee River; has 1,050 inhabitants—700 white, 350 black, 125 private dwellings, 1 hotel, 6 churches, 3 schools with 200 pupils, 2 weekly newspapers, 14 dry goods stores, 7 grocery stores, 4 physicians, 13 lawyers, 1 dentist.

Tennille, on Central Railroad, 55 miles from Macon, 136 from Savannah ; (details not reported).

WILKINSON.—Population in 1870, 9,383—4,684 white, 4,699 black ; 1½ per cent. of area too broken for profitable tillage, 2½ per cent. irreclaimable swamp, 60 per cent. of tillable land cleared, 50 per cent. sandy pine land— rest clay with oak and hickory growth ; 57½ per cent. of laborers black ; 42 public free schools for whites, 7 for blacks ; Baptists have 20 churches, Methodists 12, Episcopalians 1, Roman Catholics 1 ; flour and lumber mills are the only manufactures.

Irwinton, the capital town, is 3½ miles from the Central Railroad, 30 miles from Macon, the market town of the county; has 275 inhabitants—225 white, 50 black; 35 private dwellings, 1 hotel, 1 union church; 1 school with 50 pupils, 1 weekly newspaper, 3 dry goods stores, 6 grocery stores, 4 physicians, 8 lawyers, 2 dentists.

SOUTHEAST GEORGIA.

This division embraces 15 counties, and comprises the coast and tide-water section of the State. The entire region is tertiary and mostly without rocks. It is the last formed and first settled portion of Georgia, and its area of dry land is being gradually added to year after year through the action of the tides. It is low and level, the average elevation being less than 100 feet.

It has three distinct soils: 1, light, sandy and poor; 2, dark sandy loam containing a large amount of vegetable matter; 3, reddish and clayey. The first is naturally unproductive and covered with stunted pines and saw palmetto; but swamp muck being abundant, with a proper distribution of it over the land, it may be cultivated with reasonable success. The second variety is covered with a natural growth of yellow pine, magnolia, red bay, live-oak, cedar, and cabbage palmetto, and in productiveness is excelled by no land in the State; it has a yellow clay subsoil, varying from 10 inches to 3 feet; Sea-island cotton, corn, and sugar cane grow in the greatest luxuriance. The third variety is also very productive, pine, oak, hickory and gum being the prevailing forest growth; subsoil clay, red and yellow; average depth below the surface 8 to 12 inches. It is the great rice-producing section of the State—the broad bottoms of the Savannah, the two Ogeechees, the Altamaha, and Saltilla, being devoted almost exclusively to that cereal, It is also grown to a less extent on the St. Mary's, and considerable quantities on inland swamps, the irrigation in the latter being effected by means of "backwater," collected from rains and secured by dams. Sea-island, or long staple cotton, was the only variety formerly grown, but of late years the short staple has been introduced and cultivated with fair success. Corn, oats, pumpkins, potatoes, ground-peas all do well. The Sea-islands are devoted almost exclusively to cotton, corn, cane, fruits and vegetables. Cypress and palmetto abound in the swamps and river bottoms.

Average yield, per acre, of staple crops, with fair cultivation: Sea-island cotton, 600 lbs. in seed; corn, 15 bushels; oats, 25 bushels; rice, 40 bushels; cane syrup, 300 gallons; potatoes, 200 bushels. On best lands—1,500 lbs. seed cotton, 60 bushels rice, 600 gallons syrup, 50 bushels corn, 40 bushels oats, 400 bushels potatoes—are often produced on one acre. Corn planted middle of February till 1st of June, gathered in August and September; cotton planted March and April, gathered in autumn months; rice planted March to June, harvested last of August till 1st October; cane planted February and March, cut in October and early in November; potatoes planted March to June, gathered July to November; oats sowed in October, harvested in May.

Average wages of good farm hands, per month, with rations, $9; of ordinary mechanics, $1.50 to $2.50 per day.

The fruits best adapted to the soil and climate, are the figs, melons of all kinds, scuppernong grapes, pomegranates, sand or LeConte pears, some varieties of apples, strawberries; the orange, lemon, lime and banana, are also grown successfully.

This section exports, annually, large quantities of fruits, chiefly melons—also vegetables ; nearly every variety of the latter attains to great perfection.

The climate is delightful in winter, the mean temperature being about 48° ; nor is the heat oppressive in summer, 79° being the mean temperature. The mercury seldom rises above 90° or falls below 32°. The bracing influences of the sea-breezes is felt throughout this section. Snow is rarely seen, and never sufficient to lie on the ground half a day. Along the coast and off the fresh water rivers, the section is among the healthiest in the State.

The district is well watered by running streams, and all parts of it convenient to market. Drinking water, though not cold, is good and wholesome. Railroads penetrate every county, except two, and they are well supplied with navigable streams, connecting with inland steamboat navigation from Savannah to Florida. The pine lands of this section are well timbered, and under good culture, produce fine crops. It may be bought at from 50 cents to $2.00 per acre, and on a liberal credit ; improved lands of the second quality mentioned, are worth from $5 to $10 per acre ; good river rice lands, from $25 to $30 per acre.

In Effingham, Camden, Wayne and Charlton, there are large deposits of calcareous marl, where it can be utilized to the greatest advantage in agriculture. Our State Geologist, in commenting on this division of the State, uses the following language :

" I have seen no section of Georgia in which the people seem to secure a comfortable supply of food with less effort, and can see no reason why the whole country may not be made equal, if not superior, to that section of Prussia where Frederick the Great founded the city of Berlin. from which capital, within this decade, terms have been dictated to the continent of Europe. There is the greatest similarity in the soil and topography of the two sections, and, should the tide of German emigration be turned hither, there would soon be realized to them the comforts and pleasures of the Fatherland."

COUNTIES.

APPLING.—Population, in 1870, 5,086—4,110 white, 976 black; ten per cent. of tillable land cleared, 6 per cent irreclaimable swamp, 75 per cent of field laborers white ; public free schools for whites, 27 ; for blacks, 3 ; Baptists have 5 churches; Methodist. 10 ; 300 persons engaged in the manufacture of turpentine, rosin, etc., 100 in lumber, 200 in timber ; 1 bedstead factory, 1 chair factory.

Baxley, the capital town, is on the Macon & Brunswick Railroad, 90 miles from Savannah, 70 miles from Brunswick, 10 miles from Altamaha River ; has 275 inhabitants—200 white, 75 black ; 25 private dwellings, 1 hotel, 1 school with 25 pupils, 6 dry goods stores, 4 grocery stores, 2 physicians, 4 lawyers, 1 dentist.

BRYAN,—Population, in 1870, 5,252—1,647 white, 3,605 black ; has 15 per cent. irreclaimable swamp, 30 per cent of tillable land cleared ; 55 per cent. of farm laborers white; marls abundant ; public free schools for whites 12, for black 2 ; Baptist churches 5, Methodist 6. The rice lands of Bryan are among the most productive and valuable in the State.

Eden, the capital town, is a very small village, without business, and containing little else than a court house; is about 8 miles from the Atlantic & Gulf Railroad, and same distance from Central Railroad, 20 miles from Savannah, the market town, and 3 miles from the Cannouchee River, a navigable stream.

CAMDEN.—Population in 1870, 4.615—1,458 white, 3,157 black ; a small proportion of county irreclaimable swamp, 25 per cent. of tillable land cleared, the rice lands not excelled anywhere in the South, and are quite extensive, the average product 60 bushels per acre; marl beds of best quality exist on Satilla river ; has 11 public free schools for whites, 8 for blacks; 10 Baptist churches, 10 Methodist, 1 Episcopal, 1 Presbyterian, 1 Roman Catholic; lumber the only manufacture of county, exported in large quantities.

St. Mary's, the capital town, is situated on St. Mary's River, in sight of the ocean, 45 miles from a railroad, is the market town for the county ; has 1,200 inhabitants—550 white, 650 black, 64 private dwellings, 1 hotel, 6 churches, 5 schools with 130 pupils, 9 mixed stores, 2 physicians, 3 lawyers, several large steam lumber mills.

CHARLTON.—Population in 1870, 1,897—1,496 white, 401 black ; 33 per cent. of county, included in Okefinokee swamp, 5 per cent. of tillable land cleared 90 per cent. of farm laborers white; marls of best quality abound in the county ; public free schools 10: Methodist churches 6, Baptist 2; cotton gin factories, shingle and stave works, and lumber mills the only manufacturing establishments.

Trader's Hill, the capital town, is on the St. Mary's River, a navigable stream, 45 miles from its mouth ; has 65 inhabitants—25 white, 40 black, 12 private dwellings, 1 hotel, 1 church, school with 25 pupils, 3 dry-goods stores, 1 grocery store, 1 lawyer, no physician.

CHATHAM.—Population in 1870 41,279—16,760 white, 24,518 black; has about 10 per cent. irreclaimable swamp, 12 per cent. of tillable land cleared, 90 per cent. of farm laborers black ; chief products rice, vegetables, fruits ; about 100 public and private schools; Methodist churches 12, Baptist 14, Presbyterian 6, Episcopal 4, Roman Catholic 3, Congregational 2, Lutheran 1, Jewish Synagogues 3; manufactories—rice mills for threshing 15, capital invested $200.000, hands employed 450; rice mills for cleaning 5, capital invested $500,000, hands employed 40; agricultural implements 1, capital invested $5,000, hands employed 12 ; barrel and cask factories 2, capital $5,000, hands employed 50; flour and corn mills 5, capital $75,000, hands employed 40 ; wagon, carriage and dray factories 9, capital $75,000, hands employed 40; 1 paper mill, capital $80,000, hands employed 40; engine and car factories 2, capital $150,000, hands employed 567; 1 cotton factory, 1 fertilizer factory, 4 iron and brass foundries; 4 lumber mills, capital $50,000, hands employed 80; 4 manufactories of lumber, capital $60,000, hands employed 120.

Savannah, the capital town and first capital of the State, is situated on the bank of the river of that name, eighteen miles from its mouth, in latitude 32° 04' 52", longitude 81° 05' 26". It is the terminus of three trunk lines of railroad, and its ship tonnage, foreign and coastwise, amounted in 1877 to 1,176,562; men 31,504. It is the second cotton port in rank in the Southern States; has a population of about 28,000—15,000 white, 13,000 black; 5,600 private dwellings, 8 hotels, 34 churches, 6 banks, 1 daily newspaper, 5 weekly newspapers, 27 dry-goods stores, 217 grocery stores, 21 drug stores, 40 physicins, 64 lawyers, 10 dentists.

CLINCH.—Population, in 1870, 3,945—3,437 white, 507 black; has 18 per cent. of irreclaimable swamp, 15 per cent of tillable land cleared; soil sandy throughout; 75 per cent of farm laborers white; has 21 public free schools for whites, 1 for blacks; Baptist churches, 10; Methodist, 7; Second Adventists, 1; lumber business employs 150 hands, and naval stores 150, both interests prosperous,

Homerville, the capital town, is on Atlantic & Gulf Railroad, 122 miles from Savannah, the market town, 50 miles from navigation on Satilla River; has 400 inhabitants—250 white, 150 black; 50 private dwellings, 2 churches, 1 hotel, 2 schools with 50 pupils, 4 dry goods stores, 2 grocery stores, 2 physicians, 2 lawyers.

COFFEE.—Population in 1870, 3,192—2,514 white, 678 black; 25 per cent. of area irreclaimable swamp, 25 per cent. of tillable land cleared, 75 per cent. of field labor performed by whites; there are 20 public free schools for whites, 1 for blacks; the Baptists have 10 churches, Methodists 15, Roman Catholics 1; lumber and grist mills the only manufacturing establishments.

Douglas, the capital town, is 20 miles from a railroad, 15 from a navigable stream and 20 from the market town of the county (other details not reported.)

ECHOLS.—Population in 1870, 1,972—1,513 white, 465 black; 33 per cent. of area irreclaimable swamp, 50 per cent of tillable land cleared, 75 per cent. of farm laborers white; large beds of limestone on Alapaha River; has 13 public free schools for whites, 1 for blacks; Baptists have 7 churches, Methodists 4, Christians 1; no manufactories; county abounds in finest pine timber.

Statenville, the capital town, is 6½ miles from the Florida branch of the Atlantic & Gulf Railroad, and 20 miles from the market town; has 195 inhabitants—165 whites, 30 blacks; 10 private dwellings, 1 church, 1 hotel, 1 school with 30 pupils, 2 dry goods stores, no physicians or lawyers, 1 dentist.

EFFINGHAM.—Population in 1870, 4,214—2,507 white, 1,704 black.; about 10 per cent. of the county irreclaimable swamp, but 5 per cent. of tillable land cleared, all sandy with deep clay subsoil; abundant beds of excellent calcareous marl on Savannah river; 57 per cent. of field labor performed by whites; 10 public free schools well distributed, besides private schools; 7 Baptist churches, 5 Methodist, 5 Lutheran.

Springfield, the capital town, is six miles from Central Railroad, 12 miles from Savannah river; has 33 inhabitants—25 white, 8 black; 10 private dwellings, 2 churches, 1 school with 15 pupils, 1 dry-goods store, 1 grocery store, 1 physician, 1 lawyer.

GLYNN.—Population in 1870, 5,376—1,926 white, 3,450 black; 20 per cent. of area irreclaimable swamp, 10 per cent. of tillable land cleared; marl of excellent quality exists; 98 per cent. of farm laborers whites; public free school system is imperfectly organized; Baptist churches 4, Methodist 6, Presbyterians 1, Episcopal 1, Roman Catholic 1; lumber and naval stores are the important interests of the county, and large exports are annually made of each.

Brunswick, the capital town is situated on St. Simon's Sound, opposite the mouth of Turtle river, and is the terminus of two trunk lines of railway; i has 2,700 inhabitants—1,500 white, 1,200 black; 700 private dwellings, 2 hotels, 9 churches, 2 banks, 6 schools with 300 pupils, 1 weekly newspaper, 8 dry-goods stores, 20 grocery stores, 1 drug store, 6 physicians, 8 lawyers, 3 dentists.

LIBERTY.—Population in 1870, 7,088—2,428 white, 5,260 black; has much swamp land, but nearly all considered reclaimable; of tillable land only 10 per cent. is cleared; large deposits of marl on North Newport river near Dorchester; 75 per cent. of farm laborers black; 20 public free schools for whites, 24 for blacks; Baptist, Methodist and Presbyterian the prevailing religious sects.

Walthourville, the capital town, is situated on the Atlantic and Gulf Railroad, 38 miles from Savannah, the market town of the county; has 395 inhabitants—195 white, 200 black; 34 private dwellings, no hotel, 3 churches, 3 schools with 30 pupils, 4 mixed stores, 3 physicians, 4 lawyers.

McINTOSH.—Population in 1870, 4,484—1,196 white, 3,288 black; 15 per cent. of area irreclaimable swamp, 30 per cent. of tillable land cleared, 95 per cent. of farm laborers black; lumber mills the only manufacturing interest of the county—rice its chief agricultural product; 5 public free schools for whites, 6 for blacks; 6 Baptist churches, 5 Methodist, 2 Presbyterians, 4 Episcopal, 1 Roman Catholic.

Darien, the capital town, is situated on the Altamaha river, 4 miles from its mouth, 30 miles from Atlantic & Gulf Railroad, 60 miles from Savannah; has 7 large steam saw mills, employing 125 hands, and is the largest lumber port on the South-Atlantic coast; has 1,500 inhabitants—500 white, 1,000 black; 400 private dwellings, 1 hotel, 6 churches, 1 weekly newspaper, 2 schools, with 150 pupils, 10 dry goods stores, 15 grocery stores, 4 physicians, 5 lawyers

PIERCE.—Population in 1870, 2,788—1,964 white; 814 black; 7½ per cent. of area irreclaimable swamp, 15 per cent. of tillable land cleared, 83 per cent. of farm laborers white; lands all sandy, but swamp muck abundant and convenient; has 17 public free schools for whites, 3 for blacks; 7 Baptist churches, 3 Methodist, 1 Presbyterian; 4 steam lumber mills, employing 40 hands each, 5 turpentine distilleries, from 40 to 60 hands each.

Blackshear, the capital town, is on the Atlantic & Gulf Railroad, 86 miles from Savannah, the market town, has 800 inhabitants—425 white, 375 black; 125 private dwellings, 2 hotels, 5 churches, 5 schools with 147 pupils, 1

weekly newspaper, 7 dry goods stores, 6 grocery stores, 1 drug store, 3 physicians, 3 lawyers, 1 dentist.

WARE.—Population in 1870, 2,286—1,834 white, 452 black; about 33 per cent. of county included in Okefinokee Swamp, 10 per cent. of tillable land cleared, lands all sandy with clay subsol; large deposits of marl of excellent quality on Satilla river. 75 per cent. of farm laborers white; 18 public free schools for whites, 3 for black; 3 Baptist churches, 6 Methodist; 6 steam lumber mills and 1 turpentine distillery, employing 210 hands.

Waycross, the capital town, is situated at the intersection of the Atlantic and Gulf and the Brunswick and Albany Railroads, 95 miles from Savannah, 57 miles from Brunswick, 2 miles from Satilla river, a navigable stream, has 345 inhabitants—300 white, 45 black; 30 private dwellings, 2 hotels, 1 church, 3 schools with 40 pupils, 2 dry-goods stores, 4 grocery stores, 2 physicians. 3 lawyers, 1 dentist.

WAYNE.—Population in 1870, 2,177—1,798 white, 379 black; 10 per cent. of area irreclaimable swamp; 10 per cent. of tillable land cleared, 75 per cent. of farm laborers white; large deposits of marl of superior quality on Altamaha and Satilla Rivers, easily obtained; 25 public free schools for whites, 3 for blacks; 12 Baptist churches, 8 Methodist, 1 Presbyterian; about 250 hands employed in lumber mills, 150 in manufacture of naval stores.

Jesup, the capital town, is situated at the intersection of the Atlantic and Gulf and the Macon and Brunswick Railroads, 57 mils from Savannah, 40 miles from Brunswick; has 850 inhabitants—400 white, 450 black; 75 private dwellings, 2 hotels, 4 churches, 2 schools with 75 pupils, 1 weekly newspaper, 7 mixed stores, 1 drug store, 3 physicians, 1 lawyer.

Waynesville, the former county site, has 125 inhabitants—75 white, 50 black; 15 private residences, 2 churches, 2 stores of general merchandise.

SOUTHWEST GEORGIA.

This division is composed of thirty-three counties, and embraces all that country lying between the Ocmulgee and Allapaha Rivers in the east, and the Chattahoochee River in the west; the northern boundary being a line from Macon to Columbus, and the State of Florida its boundary in the south. Like Southeast Georgia, the entire region is tertiary. It is more broken, or rolling, than Southeast Georgia, and, with the exception of marl, buhr and limestone, is, in a great measure, destitute of rocks. It has also a greater proportion of clay lands and oak and hickory forest growth, although much the larger part of it is a light sandy soil, and was originally covered with yellow, or long-leaf pine.

The clay lands are, generally, very rich, and their fertility lasting; the pine lands produce freely, are easily worked, but are less durable, though with reasonable fertilization they last for many years. The district contains very little waste land, or lands too poor or too swampy for cultivation, while the alluvial lands of the Chattahoochee and Flint Rivers, and of many of the creeks, have made the section famous as the best cotton region of the State. Corn, oats, wheat, rye, and sugar cane grow well.

The depth of the subsoil beneath the surface, on clay lands, is 6 to 10 inches; on sandy lands, from 12 inches to 3 feet. The preponderating forest growth is long-leaf, or yellow pine, furnishing the best of lumber, large quantities of which are prepared annually for export and domestic use. The supply would seem to be almost inexhaustible. Spirits of turpentine, rosin, pitch, and tar—all the products of this tree—are made in considerable quantities, and the interest is on the increase. In the swamps and river bottoms there are cypress, cotton-wood, poplar, ash, maple, beach, birch, red-bay, magnolia, sweet-gum, and water oak ; while the growth of the clay belts is red and post oaks, black jack, hickory, walnut, black-gum, dogwood, and buck-eye.

Cotton is the leading market crop of this division, and previous to the derangement of plantation labor by emancipation, its crop of the staple probably equalled the production of all the rest of the State. Corn and oats grow to great perfection, but none for export since the war ; sugar cane is a successful crop throughout the section ; tobacco, in considerable quantities, is grown in the southern counties.

The average yields, per acre, with good cultivation, are: cotton, 500 lbs. in seed ; corn, 10 bushels ; oats, 15 bushels ; syrup, 200 gallons ; sweet potatoes, 150 bushels ; ground peas, 50 bushels. On best lands, without manure, 1,500 to 2,000 lbs. cotton in seed, 50 to 75 bushels corn, 50 to 65 bushels oats, 400 gallons of syrup, and 400 bushels sweet potatoes, are often produced. It is reliably reported that a Berrien county farmer produced 800 bushels of sweet potatoes on one acre, under high cultivation. Over 900 gallons of syrup, per acre, has been made in Thomas county.

Cotton is planted early in April, picking commences in August; corn planted in February and March, matures in August ; oats sowed usually in November, harvested last of May to last of June ; sugar cane planted February and March, cut October and November.

Average wages of good farm hands, $9 per month ; of ordinary mechanics, $1.25 to $2 per day.

The fruits best adapted to the section, are the peach, pear, melon, grape (especially the scuppernong), fig, pomegranate, some varieties of apple, strawberry ; in the southern tier of counties, the orange, lemon and banana are successfully grown. There is no country where all the vegetables grow to greater perfection when cultivated with ordinary skill. The tea-plant and the olive have also been successfully grown in this and other southern divisions of the State.

The climate varies but little from that of Southeast Georgia, the average mean temperature being, in summer, 85° ; in winter, 65° ; extremes, 94° and 32°. Snow falls about once in 10 or 15 years, never sufficient to completely cover the ground. The health of the hill-country and pine lands is good the year round, but fevers, generally of a mild type, are common along the lines of rivers and swamps in late summer and early fall months.

The country is well watered, and good water powers are found where the streams break through the marl beds, with which many of the counties abound. Several railroads traverse the section, while the Ocmulgee, Flint, and Chattahoochee Rivers furnish transportation nearly the entire year.

The poorer, unimproved pine lands, well timbered, may be bought at 50 cents per acre; good at $1 to $2.50; best lands at from $4 to $10—all on a liberal credit.

The drinking water in the hill country is good, though not very cold; in the flat lands not so good, and generally impregnated with lime. The waters abound with fish, and the forests furnish game, large and small, in any quantity desired.

The large bodies of unimproved land, to be found in nearly every county of the district, furnish excellent pasturage the year round for cattle and sheep, and are free to all. Little or no feeding or sheltering is required, and beef and mutton are taken directly from the range to market.

COUNTIES.

BAKER.—Population in 1870, 6,843—1,888 white, 4,955 black; 7 per cent. of area irreclaimable swamp, 45 per cent of tillable land cleared, 75 per cent. of field laborers black; limestone, composed chiefly of shells, abundant; 10 public free schools for whites, 8 for blacks; Baptist churches, 5; Methodist, 3; Presbyterian, 1; flour and lumber mills the only manufactories.

Newton, the capital town, is situated on Flint River, 8 miles from South Ga., & Florida Railroad, and 20 miles from Albany, the market town of the county (other details not reported).

BERRIEN.—Population in 1870, 4,518—4,057 white, 400 black; 15 per cent. of its area is irreclaimable swamp, 10 per cent. of tillable land cleared, soil all sandy with yellowish clay subsoil 6 to 10 inches below surface, original forest all pine; 87 per cent. of field laborers white; has 29 public free schools, all for whites; Baptist churches 11, Methodist 6, Roman Catholic 1; 1 buggy, wagon and furniture factory, employing 50 hands; flour and lumber mills are the other manufactures.

Nashville, the capital town, is 12 miles from the Brunswick and Albany Railroad, 40 miles from a navigable stream, 12 miles from the market town of the county; has 203 inhabitants—200 white, 3 black, 30 private dwellings, 1 hotel, 2 churches. 2 schools with 40 pupils, 1 dry goods store, 1 grocery store, 2 physicians, 3 lawyers, 1 dentist.

BIBB.—Population in 1870, 21,255—9,831 white, 11,424 black; 10 per cent. of area irreclaimable swamp, 80 per cent. of tillable land cleared, 70 per cent. sandy soil; 90 per cent. of farm laborers black; has 38 public free schools, with nearly 1,600 white pupils and about the same of black, 2 male colleges, 1 female college, numerous private schools; 6 Baptist churches, 8 Methodist, 3 Presbyterian, 4 Episcopal, 1 Roman Catholic, 1 Jewish synagogue; 2 cotton factories; 3 railroad car factories, 7 iron foundries, 1 brass foundry, 3 cotton gin factories, with numerous flour and lumber mills.

Macon, the capital town, is situated at the head of navigation on the Ocmulgee river, is the market town of a large district of country; has, with the suburb of Vineville, 12,000 inhabitants—8,000 white, 4,000 black; 4 banks, 2,000 private dwellings, 4 hotels, 21 churches, 2 male colleges, 1 female college, 1 high school, 6 public grammar schools, 1 academy for the blind, 1 medical college, 1 daily and 2 weekly newspapers, 2 cotton factories, 7 iron foundries, 2 cotton gin factories, 3 railroad car factories, about 30 dry goods stores, 6 grocery stores, 7 shoe stores, 3 hardware stores, 2 crockery stores, 10 drug stores, 27 physicians, 42 lawyers, 5 dentists.

Brooks.—Population in 1870, 8,342—4,111 white, 4,231 black; 10 per cent. of area irreclaimable swamp, 37 per cent. of tillable land cleared, 80 per cent. sandy soil, 62 per cent. of farm laborers black; 26 public free schools for whites, 13 for blacks; Baptist churches 14, Methodist 10, Presbyterian 2, Episcopal 1; 1 cotton factory with 40 operatives, 2 turpentine distilleries, flour and lumber mills in sufficient number.

Quitman, the capital town, is on the Atlantic and Gulf Railroad, 175 miles from Savannah, and is the market town of county; has 2,000 inhabitants—1,200 white, 800 black; 400 private dwellings, 3 hotels, 5 churches, 2 schools with 150 pupils, 2 weekly newspapers, 20 dry-goods stores, 3 grocery stores, 2 drug stores, 2 physicians, 6 lawyers, 2 dentists, 1 cotton factory.

Calhoun.—Population in 1870, 5,503—2,026 white, 3,477 black; 5 per cent. of area is irreclaimable swamp, 53 per cent. sandy soil with pine forest growth, 42 per cent. of tillable land cleared, 78 per cent. of farm labor performed by blacks; has 12 public free schools for whi es, 9 for blacks; Baptists have 11 churches, Methodists 8, Presbyterians 1: county well supplied with railroad transportation; flour and lumber are the only manufactures.

Morgan, the capital town, is 4½ miles from a railroad, 25 miles from a navigable stream, 30 miles from Albany, the market town of the section, though much produce is sold in the county; has 119 inhabitants—84 white, 35 black; 22 private dwellings, 2 churches, 1 school with 20 pupils, 1 hotel, 2 dry-goods stores, 1 grocery store, 1 physician, 4 lawyers.

Chattahoochee.—Population in 1370, 6,059—2,654 white, 3,504 black; entire area considered tillable, 75 per cent. sandy pine land, 60 per cent. cleared, 66 per cent. of farm laborers black; several large deposits of marl of best quality, containing over 30 per cent. of lime; has 14 public free schools, all for whites; 5 Baptist churches, 5 Methodist; no manufactures except flour and lumber; Chattahoochee river, navigable, forms the western boundary.

Ousseta, the capital town, is 20 miles from Columbus, the market town of the county; has 175 inhabitants—110 white, 65 black, 32 private dwellings, 1 hotel, 4 churches, 2 schools with 60 scholars, 2 mixed stores, 1 physician, 3 lawyers.

Clay.—Population, in 1870, 5,493—2,644 white, 2,849 black; no waste land in county, 60 per cent. sandy with pine forest growth, 38 per cent. cleared, 66 per cent. of farm laborers black; large and valuable marl beds on the Chattahoochee River and tributaries; has 14 public free schools for whites, 2 for blacks; 9 Baptist churches, 6 Methodist, 2 Presbyterian, 10 Baptist and Methodist churches for negroes; no manufactures except flour and lumber.

Fort Gaines, the capital town, is situated on the Chattahoochee River, and is the terminus of a railroad and market town of county; has 1,000 inhabitants—600 white, 400 black; 174 private dwellings, 2 hotels, 5 churches, 3 schools with 110 pupils, 1 weekly newspaper, 11 dry-goods stores, 16 grocery stores, 2 physicians, 3 lawyers.

Colquitt—Population in 1870, 1,654—1,517 white, 137 black; 1 per cent. of county irreclaimable swamp, 66 per cent. sandy pine land, only 7 per land cleared; 96 per cent. of farm laborers white; large and valuable deposits of marl on Oclockonee River, which runs through county; has 13 public free schools, all for whites; 15 Baptist churches, 10 Methodist, 1 Presbyterian, 1 Episcopal; no manufactures.

Moultrie, the capital town, is 25 miles from a railroad, 35 miles from a navigable stream, 28 miles from Thomasville; 38 miles from Albany, the market towns; has 27 inhabitants—all white, 5 private dwellings, no hotels or churches, 1 school with 15 pupils, 1 dry goods store, 1 grocery store.

CRAWFORD—Population, in 1870, 7,557—3,284 white, 4,273 black ;' nearly whole area reported tillable; 70 per cent. clay soil, 40 per cent. cleared, 60 per cent. of farm laborers black ; considerable deposits of marl in southern portion of county, 5 miles from county site; has 22 public free schools for whites, 8 for blacks; 8 Baptist churches, 10 Methodist, about 15 churches for blacks; water-powers excellent, and flour and lumber mills abundant; 3 potteries employ 11 hands.

Knoxville, the capital town, is 13 miles from Southwestern Railroad, 25 miles from Macon, the market town and a navigable stream ; has 155 inhabitants—115 white, 40 black ; 25 private dwellings, 1 hotel, 2 churches, 1 school with 20 pupils 4 stores of mixed merchandise, 1 drug store, 2 physicians, 3 lawyers, 1 dentist.

DECATUR.—Is the extreme southwestern county of the State, and banner cotton county, her crop in 1869—the last reported—being 19,600 bales ; population in 1870, 15,183—7,475 white, 7,718 black ; 1 per cent. of area irreclaimable swamp, 10 per cent. of tillable land cleared, 50 per cent. clay soil, rest sandy with good clay subsoil and heavily timbered with pine ; 75 per cent. of farm laborers black; large deposits of marl in the county, and limestone of good quality abundant; has 37 public free schools for whites, 21 for blacks: 15 Baptist churches, 15 Methodist, 5 Presbyterian, 1 Episcopal; 1 large cotton factory (now suspended); flour and lumber mills abundant.

Bainbridge, the capital town, is situated on the Flint river, 20 miles from its mouth ; is the terminus of the Atlantic and Gulf Railroad, 237 miles from Savannah ; has 2,000 inhabitants—1,200 white, 800 black, 300 private dwellings, 2 hotels, 6 churches, 1 bank, 3 schools with 125 scholars, 1 weekly newspaper, 12 dry-goods stores, 4 grocery stores, 1 drug store, 4 physicians, 13 lawyers, 1 dentist.

DOOLY.—Population in 1870, 9,790—4,935 white, 4,855 black ; 2½ per cent. of area irreclaimable swamp, only 3½ per cent. clay soil, rest sandy, 28 per cent. of tillable land cleared, 70 per cent. of farm laborers black ; large deposits of marl convenient for agricultural purposes; has 37 public free schools for whites, 7 for blacks; 18 Baptist churches, 8 Methodist, 1 Universalist; corn, flour and lumber mills sufficient.

Vienna, the capital town, is 22 miles from a railroad, 25 miles from a navigable stream, 25 miles from the market town; has 294 inhabitants—175 white, 119 black, 59 private residences, 1 hotel, 4 churches, 1 school with 60 scholars, 4 dry-goods stores, 5 grocery stores, 3 physicians, 9 lawyers.

DOUGHERTY.—Population in 1870, 11,517—2,093 white, 9,424 black ; about

10 per cent. of area irreclaimable swamp, 40 per cent. clay soil of best quality, rest sandy with pine forest; 75 per cent. of tillable land cleared, 95 per cent. of farm laborers black; large deposits of marl valuable for agricultural purposes, has 8 public free schools for whites, 25 for blacks, 1,615 pupils, also private schools at county site; Baptist churches 8, Methodist 3, Presbyterian 1, Roman Catholic 1, Jewish synagogue 1. Dougherty ranks among the best planting counties of the State.

Albany, the capital town, is situated on Flint River, at the head of navigation, and is the terminus of four railroads; is 104 miles from Macon, and the market town of a large district of surrounding country; has 3,300 inhabitants—1,700 white, 1,600 black, 270 private dwellings, 2 hotels, 8 churches, 1 bank, 9 schools with 480 pupils, 2 weekly newspapers, 67 stores of mixed merchandise, 7 physicians, 11 lawyers, 2 dentists.

EARLY.—Population in 1870, 6,998—2,820 white, 4,172 black; 5 per cent. of area irreclaimable swamp; 20 per cent. of tillable land cleared, 74 per cent. sandy pine land, 75 per cent. of farm laborers black; extensive deposits of marl of excellent quality and available for agricultural purposes; has 25 public free schools for whites, 17 for blacks; 12 Baptist and 12 Methodist churches; 1 cotton factory for spinning yarns with 40 operatives, flour and lumber mills sufficient; timber of best quality.

Blakely, the capital town, is on a line of located railroad completed to a point only 9 miles distant, 9 miles from the Chattahoochee River, and is the market town of the county; has 700 inhabitants—400 white, 300 black; 60 private dwellings, 1 hotel, 4 churches, 3 schools with 125 scholars, 1 weekly newspaper, 4 dry-goods stores, 2 grocery stores, 1 drug store, 4 physicians, 3 lawyers, 2 dentists.

HOUSTON.—Population in 1870, 20,406—5,071 white, 15,332 black; 2 per cent of area irreclaimable swamp, 50 per cent. of clay soil, 64 per cent. of tillable land cleared, 75 per cent. of farm laborers black; a high limestone ridge, ½ mile to 2 miles wide, extending across county from the Ocmulgee to the Flint Rivers contains immense beds of calcareous marl which has been used with good effect on lands; also, several deposits of green sand, very valuable as a fertilizer; 33 public free schools for whites, 27 for blacks; 20 Baptist churches, 25 Methodist, 2 Presbyterian, 5 Primitive Baptists, also Lutheran and Bible Christian congregations; 1 cotton factory with 75 operatives near Perry; large agricultural works at Fort Valley; 1 cotton gin factory, together with flour and saw mills well distributed over country.

Perry, the capital town, is the terminus of a branch railroad from the Southwestern Railroad at Fort Valley, 11 miles long, about midway (15 miles) between the Ocmulgee and Flint rivers; 28 miles from Macon, the market town of county; has 1,700 inhabitants—1,000 white, 700 black; 80 private dwellings, 1 hotel, 4 churches, 4 schools with 150 pupils, 1 weekly newspaper, 7 dry goods stores, 10 grocery stores, 1 drug store, 4 physicians, 9 lawyers, 1 dentist.

Fort Valley, on Southwestern Railroad, 25 miles from Macon, has 1,800 inhabitants—1,000 white, 800 black; 140 private dwellings, 1 hotel, 6 churches, 7 schools with 175 pupils, 1 weekly newspaper, 1 bank, 13 dry goods stores, 8 grocery stores, 1 drug store, 5 physicians, 5 lawyers, 1 dentist.

IRWIN—Population, in 1870, 1,837—1,541 white, 296 black ; about 15 per cent. of area irreclaimable swamp, only 5 per cent. of tillable land cleared, whole county sandy pine land, 75 per cent. of farm laborers white; has 13 public free schools for whites, 1 for blacks; 8 Baptist churches, 4 Methodist stock range excellent, and much attention is given to cattle and sheep.

Irwinville, the capital town, is a small village, 20 miles from the Brunswick and Albany Railroad, same distance from a navigable stream ; has 12 inhabitants—6 white, 6 black ; 2 private dwelling one of which is used as a hotel, no church, 1 school, with 13 pupils, 1 dry goods store.

LEE—Population, in 1870, 9,567—1,924 white, 7,643 black ; 90 per cent. of area sandy, with heavy pine forest growth, but very little irreclaimable swamp, about 50 per cent of the county cleared ; 95 per cent. of farm laborers black ; has one large deposit of marl, which has been used with good effect in agriculture ; has 17 public free schools for whites, 12 for blacks ; 7 Baptist churches, 6 Methodist, 1 Presbyterian ; no manufactures except flour and lumber.

Leesburg, the capital town, is on the Southwestern Railroad, 10 miles from Albany, the market town, 94 miles from Macon; other details not reported.

LOWNDES—Population, in 1870, 8,321—4,276 white, 4,045 black, about 1 per cent. of area irreclaimable swamp, 95 per cent. sandy soil, 90 per cent. of farm laborers black ; has 16 public free schools for whites, 10 for blacks ; 18 Baptist churches, 9 Methodist, 1 Presbyterian ; no manufactures.

Valdosta, the capital town, is situated on the Atlantic and Gulf Railroad, 164 miles from Savannah, the market town of the county ; has 2,000 inhabitants—1,200 white, 800 black ; 8 churches, 2 hotels, 2 schools with 185 pupils, 1 weekly newspaper, 15 dry goods stores, 4 grocery stores, 1 drug store, 3 physicians, 6 lawyers, 2 dentists.

MACON—Population, in 1870, 11,458—3,975 white, 7,483 black ; 10 per cent of area irreclaimable swamp, 75 per cent. sandy soil, 52 per cent. cleared ; 75 per cent. of farm laborers black ; has 28 public free schools for whites, 17 for blacks ; 13 Baptist churches, 10 Methodist, 1 Lutheran ; no manufactures except flour and lumber.

Oglethorpe, the capital town, is situated on Flint River, and on the line of Southwestern Railroad 50 miles from Macon ; has 290 inhabitants—150 white, 140 black, 50 private dwellings, 1 hotel, 4 churches, 2 schools with 50 pupils, 4 dry goods stores, 3 grocery stores, 1 drug store, 4 physicians, 3 lawyers.

Montezuma, also on line of Southwestern Railroad and Flint River, 49 miles from Macon ; is a place of considerable trade; has 2 banks, 350 inhabitants—200 white, 150 black ; 70 private dwellings, 2 hotels, 2 churches, 2 schools with 55 pupils, 1 weekly newspaper, 8 dry goods stores, 4 grocery stores, 1 drug store, 3 physicians, 4 lawyers.

Marshallville is also on line of Southwestern Railroad, 32 miles from Macon; has 400 inhabitants—200 white, 250 black, 35 private dwellings, 3 schools with 65 pupils, 3 dry-goods stores, 2 grocery stores, 1 drug store, 3 physicians, 2 lawyers, 1 dentist.

MARION.—Population in 1870, 8,000—4,169 white, 3,831 black; 5 per cent. cent. of area too hilly for successful cultivation, 1 per cent. irreclaimable swamy, 50 per cent. clay, the remainder sandy soil, 75 per cent. of tillable land cleared, 78 per cent. of farm laborers black; marl exists in two considerable deposits; has 22 public free schools for whites, 6 for blacks; 8 Methodist churches, 5 Baptist, 1 Presbyterian ; flour and lumber are the manufactures of county.

Buena Vista, the capital town, is 20 miles from the Muscogee Railroad, 30 miles from Columbus, the market town of the county, 28 miles from Southwestern Railroad; has 650 inhabitants—350 white, 300 black, 65 private dwellings, 1 hotel, 5 churches, 2 schools with 120 pupils, 1 weekly newspaper, 4 dry-goods and mixed stores, 1 grocery store, 1 drug store, 4 physicians, 6 lawyers, 1 dentist.

MILLER—Population in 1870, 3,091—2,135 white, 956 black ; 5 per cent. of area irreclaimable swamp, 75 per cent. sandy pine land, 15 per cent. of tillable land cleared, 75 per cent. of farm laborers white ; has 14 public free schools for whites, 1 for blacks ; 7 Baptist churches, 4 Methodist; flour and lumber mills; timber large and of best quality ; some beds of marl exist.

Colquitt, the capital town, is 20 miles from Bainbridge (the market town) and Flint River, 20 miles from Chattahoochee River; the Bainbridge and Cuthbert Railroad graded to the town ; population 130—white 110, black 20 ; 22 private dwellings, 1 hotel, 2 churches, 1 school, 4 dry-goods stores, 2 grocery stores, 1 drug store, 2 physicians, 3 lawyers.

MITCHELL.—Population in 1870, 6,633—3,683 white, 2,950 black ; 3 per cent. of area irreclaimable swamp, 80 per cent. sandy pine land, 33 per cent. cleared, remainder heavily timbered; 75 per cent. of farm laborers black; has 23 public free schools for whites, 8 for blacks; 9 Baptist churches, 6 Methodist, 1 Presbyterian ; range for cattle and sheep unsurpassed.

Camilla, the capital town, is on the Albany branch of the Atlantic and Gulf Railroad, 24 miles from Albany, the market town of the county, and 36 miles from Bainbridge; has 1,000 inhabitants—600 white, 400 black, 150 private dwellings, 4 churches, 2 hotels, 4 schools with 150 pupils, 1 weekly newspaper, 11 dry goods stores, 3 grocery stores, 2 drug stores, 3 physicians; 8 lawyers, 1 dentist.

MUSCOGEE.—Population in 1870, 16,663—7,441 white, 9,220 black ; ⅓ of one per cent. too hilly for successful tillage; no irreclaimable swamp, 49 per cent. clay soil, remainder sandy ; 85 per cent. of farm laborers black ; marl abundant on Chattahoochee River in the southwestern part of the county ; has 14 free public schools for whites, and 12 for blacks outside city of Columbus; 10 Baptist churches, 17 Methodist, 1 Presbyterian, 1 Episcopal, 1 Roman Catholic ; 6 large cotton factories, 1 bagging factory, 1 trunk factory, 1 clothing factory, several large merchant flour mills, and lumber and corn mills.

Columbus, the capital town, is situated at the head of navigation on the Chattahoochee River, and is the terminus of 4 railroads ; has about 10,000 inhabitants—5,500 white, 4,500 black ; 1,000 private dwellings, 3 hotels, 4 banks, 12 schools with about 1,500 pupils, 2 daily newspapers, 25 dry goods stores, 125 grocery and variety stores, 5 drug stores, 15 physicians, 24 lawyers, 5 dentists.

The principal manufacturing establishments of the city are as follows :

Eagle and Phœnix Manufacturing Company, manufactures woollen and cotton goods; has 43,812 spindles, 1,600 looms, 1,800 operatives; capital $1,250,000—power, water.

Columbus Manufacturing Company—sheetings and brown domestics; 4,156 spindles, 116 looms, 135 operatives; capital $263,000—power, water.

Muscogee Manufacturing Company—cottonades, rope and domestics; 4,000 spindles, 80 looms, 130 operatives; capital $157,000—power, water.

A. Clegg & Co.—checks and stripes; 36 looms, 25 operatives; capital $10,000—power, steam.

Steam Cotton Mills—yarns and thread; 2,200 spindles, 75 operatives; capital $30,000—power, steam.

Hind & Preer—jute bagging; 15 looms, 50 operatives; capital $30,000—power, steam.

Empire Flour Mills—flour and meal; 6 Buhr runners; capacity, 250 barrels flour, 1,200 bushels meal per day ; 15 operatives; capital $50,000—power, steam.

City Mills—flour and meal; capacity, 150 barrels flour, 800 bushels meal per day; 8 operatives; capital $95,000—power, water.

Columbus Iron Works—engines, boilers, castings and machinery; 250 operatives; capital $100,000—power, steam.

Peacock's Clothing Factory; 25 operatives; capital $5,000.

Southern Plough Company—ploughs, etc.; employs 18 hands; capital $20,000—power, steam.

QUITMAN—Population, in 1870, 4,150—1,773 white, 2,337 black; about ½ of 1 per cent., of area irreclaimable swamp, 38 per cent. clay soil, remainder sandy, 64 per cent. of tillable land cleared, 78 per cent. of farm laborers black ; blue marl of excellent quality abounds on the water courses, also a black muck, both valuable as fertilizers; has 7 public free schools for whites, 4 for blacks ; 7 Baptist churches, 7 Methodist; flour and lumber are the only manufactures.

Georgetown, the capital town, is on the Southwestern Railroad and Chattahoochee River, two miles from Eufaula, Ala., the market town of the county ; has 350 inhabitants—150 white, 200 black , 40 private dwellings, 1 hotel, 1 bank, 3 churches, 3 schools with 100 pupils, 5 dry goods stores, 7 grocery stores, 1 drug store, 1 physician, 4 lawyers.

RANDOLPH.—Population in 1870, 10,561—5,084 white, 5,477 black; 8 per cent. of area irreclaimable swamp, 60 per cent. clay soil, 60 per cent. of tillable land cleared, 75 per cent. of farm laborers black ; several deposits of marl exist; has 27 public free schools for whites, 15 for blacks, 4 Baptist churches, 9 Methodist, 1 Presbyterian, 3 Primitive Baptist.

Cuthbert, the capital town is on the Southwestern Railroad, 20 miles from the Chattahoochee River; has 3,000 inhabitants—2,000 white, 1,000 black ; 625 private dwellings, 2 hotels, 1 bank, 6 churches, 6 schools with 250 pupils, 2 weekly newspapers, 10 dry-goods stores ; 8 grocery stores, 3 drug stores, 6 physician, 10 lawyers, 2 dentists.

7

Schley.—Population in 1870, 5,129—2,278 white, 2,851 black; ½ of one per cent. too hilly for successful tillage, same quantity irreclaimable swamp, 60 per cent. clay soil, remainder sandy, 72 per cent. of tillable land cleared, 63 per cent. of farm laborers black; marl beds in northern part of the county; has 11 public free schools for whites, 9 for blacks; 6 Methodist churches, 5 Baptist, 1 Universalist, flour and lumber are the manufactures.

Ellaville, the capital town, is 11 miles from Southwestern Railroad, and from Americus, the market town of the county, 40 miles from the head of navigation on Flint River; has 132 inhabitants—87 white, 45 black, 20 private dwellings, 2 churches, 2 schools with 40 pupils, 1 hotel, 1 dry-goods store, 3 grocery stores, 1 drug store, 2 physicians, 6 lawyers, 1 dentist.

Stewart.—Population in 1870, 14,204—5,104 white, 9,100 black; 2½ per cent. of area too broken for successful tillage, 1 per cent. irreclaimable swamp, 23 per cent. clay soil, remainder sandy pine land, 75 per cent. of tillable land cleared, 70 per cent. of farm laborers black; has large marl deposits, and two beds of green sand; 27 public free schools for whites, 19 for blacks; 11 Baptist churches, 10 Methodist; 1 Presbyterian, 1 Primitive Baptist, 1 Bible Christian; 1 carriage factory, and flour and lumber mills.

Lumpkin, the capital town, is 22 miles from the Southwestern Railroad, 15 miles from the Chattahoochee River, 25 from Eufaula, Ala., 36 from Columbus, and 22 from Cuthbert, all of which are market towns of the county; has 800 inhabitants—400 white, 400 black; 150 private residences, 1 hotel, 1 weekly newspaper, 5 churches, 1 school with 50 pupils, 3 dry goods stores, 4 grocery stores, 2 drug stores, 4 physicians, 8 lawyers, 1 dentist.

Sumter.—Population in 1870, 16,559—5,920 white, 10,639 black; 3 per cent. of area irreclaimable swamp, 27 per cent. clay soil, remainder sandy with original forest of pine; 46 per cent. of tillable land cleared, 82 per cent. of farm laborers black; large deposits of marl on Flint River and Line Creek; has 31 public free schools for whites, 19 for blacks; 12 Baptist churches, 11 Methodist, 2 Presbyterian, 1 Episcopal, 5 Primitive Baptist, 30 churches for blacks; 1 boot and shoe factory 20 operatives; 1 door, sash and blind factory, 15 operative; several carriage factories, and flour and lumber mills.

Americus, the capital town, is on the Southwestern Railroad, and is the market town of the county; is 72 miles from Macon, 40 miles from a navigable stream; has 6,000 inhabitants—3,000 white, 3,000 black, 700 private dwellings, 2 hotels, 3 banks, 7 churches, 10 schools with 200 pupils, 1 tri-weekly and weekly newspaper, 11 dry-goods stores, 21 grocery stores, 4 drug stores, 11 physicians, 21 lawyers, 2 dentists.

Taylor—Population, in 1870, 7,143—4,181 white, 2,962 black; 1 per cent. of area irreclaimable swamp, soil all sandy with yellow pine and blackjack forest growth, 10 per cent. of tillable land cleared; 50 per cent. of farm laborers white; has 24 public free schools for whites, 7 for blacks; 8 Baptist churches, 13 Methodist, 1 Presbyterian; 1 cotton factory with wool-carding machine attached, 50 operatives.

Butler, the capital town, is on the Southwestern Railroad, 50 miles from Macon, same distance from Columbus; is the principal market town of the county; has 700 inhabitants—500 white, 200 black; 150 private dwellings,

1 hotel, 4 churches, 4 schools with 150 pupils, 5 dry goods stores, 3 grocery stores, 1 drug store. 2 physicians, 4 lawyers, 1 dentist.

TERRELL—Population, in 1870, 9,053—3,769 white, 5,284 black ; 4 per cent of area irreclaimable swamp, soil half clay, half sandy, 32½ per cent. of tillable land cleared, 80 per cent. of farm laborers black ; limestone abundant and used by planters with good effect ; has 28 public free schools for whites, 8 for blacks ; 12 Baptist churches, 10 Methodist, 1 Presbyterian ; 1 railroad car factory with 100 hands, wagon and barrel factories and flour and lumber mills.

Dawson, the capital town, is on the Southwestern Railroad, 40 miles from Eufaula, Ala., and is the market town for most of the county products ; has 1,150 inhabitants—750 white, 400 black ; 200 private dwellings, 2 hotels, 2 banks, 4 churches, 6 schools with 225 pupils. 1 weekly newspaper, 11 dry goods stores, 9 grocery stores, 2 drug stores, 2 hardware stores, 6 physicians, 7 lawyers, 1 dentist.

THOMAS—Population in 1870, 14,523—6,160 white, 8, 363 black ; about 2 per cent of area irreclaimable swamp, 75 per cent. clay soil, 33 per cent. of tillable land cleared ; 75 per cent. of farm laborers black ; several lime deposits that might be utilized for agricultural purposes; has 33 free public schools for whites, 19 for blacks; 13 Baptist churches, 14 Methodist, 3 Presbyterian, 1 Episcopal; 1 cigar factory, 1 iron foundry, many lumber and flour mills ; is one of the most productive and prosperous counties of the State.

Thomasville, the capital town, is on the Atlantic and Gulf Railroad, 200 miles from Savannah, 37 from Bainbridge, and 60 from Albany, and is the market town of Thomas and adjoining counties ; has about 3,500 inhabitants—2,333 white, 1,167 black ; about 600 private dwellings, 2 hotels, 2 banks, 6 churches, 4 schools, 2 weekly newspapers, about 60 stores of mixed merchandise, 3 drug stores, 7 physicians, 17 lawyers, 2 dentists.

WEBSTER—Population in 1870, 4,677—2,439 white, 2,238 black ; 4 per cent. of its area irreclaimable swamp, 26 per cent. clay soil, remainder sandy soil with red and yellow clay subsoil; 60 per cent. of tillable land cleared, 58 per cent of farm laborers black ; has 15 public free schools for whites, 4 for blacks ; 5 Baptist churches, 4 Methodist, 1 Presbyterian, 3 Primitive Baptist ; tanneries, shoe shops, flour and lumber mills constitute the manufacturing interests.

Preston, the capital town, is 18 miles from Southwestern railroad and Americus, the market town; 40 miles from the Chattahoochee River ; has 131 inhabitants—72 white, 59 black ; 24 private dwellings, 1 hotel, 2 churches, 1 school with 18 pupils, 4 dry goods stores, 3 grocery stores, 1 physician, 2 lawyers,

WILCOX—Population in 1870, 2,439—1,902 white, 537 black ; 2½ per cent. of its area too broken for successful cultivation, 8 per cent, irreclaimable swamp, 25 per cent. clay soil, remainder sandy pine land, 15 per cent of tillable land cleared ; 50 per cent. of farm laborers white ; has 18 public free schools for whites, 1 for blacks ; 10 Baptist churches, 5 Methodist ; no manufactures except flour and lumber.

Abbeville, the capital town, is on the Ocmulgee River, 18 miles from Macon and Brunswick Railroad, 25 miles from Hawkinsville, the market town ; has 75 inhabitants—50 white, 25 black; 25 private dwellings, 1 hotel, 2 churches, 1 school with 25 scholars, 3 dry-goods stores, 4 grocery stores, 1 drug store, 1 physician, 1 lawyer, 1 dentist.

WORTH.—Population in 1870, 3,778—2,673 white, 1,105 black; 1¼ per cent. of area irreclaimable swamp, 15 per cent clay soil—remainder sandy with original pine forest, 20 per cent. of tillable land cleared, 58 per cent. of farm laborers white; extensive deposits of marl; has 24 public free schools for whites, 3 for blacks; 12 Baptist churches, 4 Methodist; naval stores—turpentine and rosin—the chief manufacures, flour and lumber mills equal to the demand.

Isabella, the capital town, is 2½ miles from the Brunswick and Albany Railroad, 18 miles from Flint River and Albany, the market town; has 115 inhabitants—100 white, 15 black, 25 private dwellings, 1 church, 1 hotel, 1 school with 25 pupils, 1 dry-goods store, 1 grocery store, 1 physician, 3 lawyers.

VALUABLE MINERALS.

Georgia is rich in mineral wealth, and these riches have been but partially explored. Almost every county has some valuable mineral deposit. The following list, showing the counties in which they are found, is furnished by Dr. George Little, the State Geologist. It is, therefore, official and reliable :

GOLD—is found in the following counties, viz :

Banks,	Douglas,	Hall,	Meriwether,	Rabun,
Bartow,	Elbert,	Haralson,	Milton,	Rockdale,
Bibb,	Fannin,	Harris,	Monroe,	Spalding,
Butts,	Forsyth,	Hart,	Morgan,	Taliaferro,
Campbell,	Franklin,	Heard,	Murray,	Towns,
Carroll,	Fulton,	Jackson,,	Newton,	Troup,
Cherokee,	Gilmer,	Jasper,	Oconee,	Union,
Clarke,	Glascock,	Lincoln,	Oglethorpe,	Upson,
Cobb,	Greene,	Lumpkin,	Paulding,	Walton,
Coweta,	Gwinnett,	Madison,	Pike,	White,
Dawson,	Habersham,	McDuffie,	Putnam,	Wilkes.
DeKalb,				

COPPER—is found in the following counties :

Carroll,	Fannin,	Haralson,	Milton,	Paulding,
Cherokee,	Fulton,	Lincoln,	Murray,	Towns.
Cobb,	Greene,	Lumpkin,		

MANGANESE—is found in the following counties :

Bartow,	Lincoln,	Polk,	Towns.

ASBESTUS—is found in the following counties :

Bartow,	Douglas,	Hall,	Paulding,	Towns,
Coweta,	Fulton,	Heard,	Rabun,	Troup.
DeKalb,	Habersham			

SLATE—is found in the following counties:

| Bartow, | Gordon, | Polk. |

IRON—is found in the following counties:

Banks,	Dade,	Habersham,	Milton (mag-	Troup,
Bartow,	DeKalb,	Hall,	netic),	Upson,
Burke,	Elbert,	Haralson,	Monroe,	Walker,
Catoosa (red	Fannin,	Harris,	Oconee,	Walton,
and brown	Floyd (red	Hart,	Pike,	Warren,
hematite),	and brown	Jackson,	Polk,	Webster,
Carroll,	hematite),	Jasper,	Putnam,	White,
Chattooga,	Gilmer,	Lumpkin,	Spalding,	Whitefield (red
Cherokee,	Gordon,	McDuffie,	Stewart,	and brown
Cobb,	Greene,	Meriwether,	Talbot,	hematite).

MICA—is found in the following counties:

| Carroll, | Hall, | Jasper, | Pickens, | Towns. |
| Cherokee. | | | | |

DIAMONDS, PRECIOUS STONES, GEMS, etc., are found in the following counties:

Berrien, Chalcedony,	Hall, Diamond,	Pickens, Amethyst,
Bullock, Opal,	Henry, Tourmaline,	Rabun { Corundum, Amethyst,
Carroll, Corundum,	Lincoln, Rutile,	
Cobb, Amethyst,	Lowndes, Chalcedony,	Towns { Corundum, Ruby,
DeKalb, Tourmaline,	Madison, Tourmaline,	
Douglas, Corundum,	Meriwether, Beryl,	Troup, Tourmaline,
Forsyth, Amethyst,	Newton, Beryl,	Union, Corundum,
Franklin, Tourmaline,	Oconee { Tourmaline, Beryl,	Upson, Tourmaline,
Fulton, Tourmaline,		Washington, Opal,
Gwinnett { Sm'ky Qu'rtz, Tourmaline,	Oglethorpe, Amethyst,	White, Diamond.

GALENA—is found in the following counties:

| Catoosa, | Habersham, | Lincoln, | Union. |
| Floyd, | Hall, | Murray, | |

SILVER is found in the following counties, and perhaps in some others, though it is not known that it exists in paying quantities:

| Hall, | Murray. | Union. |

GRAPHITE—is found in—

| Carroll, | Clarke, | Elbert, | Hart, | Meriwether. |
| Cherokee, | Douglas, | Habersham, | Heard, | |

KAOLIN—is found in—

| Cherokee, | Columbia, | Pickens, | Richmond. |

FIRE CLAY—is found in—

| Baldwin, | McDuffie, | Richmond. |

LIMESTONE—is found in the following counties: where it exists in the form of calcite, it is so designated:

Baker,	Dade (calcite),	Gwinnett,	Lee,	Sumter,
Bartow,	Decatur,	Habersham,	Lowndes,	Thomas,
Brooks,	Dooly,	Hall,	Mitchell,	Twiggs (cal.),
Calhoun,	Dougherty,	Houston,	Macon,	Walker (cal.),
Catoosa,	Floyd,	Irwin,	Polk,	Wilcox,
Chattooga,	Gordon,	Jefferson(cal.),	Randolph(cal),	Whitefield(cal.)
Clay,				

BUHRSTONE—is found in—

Appling,	Decatur,	Laurens,	Randolph,	Terrell,
Baker,	Dooly,	Lee,	Screven,	Twiggs,
Bibb,	Dougherty,	Miller,	Sumter,	Webster,
Bulloch,	Early,	Pulaski,	Tatnall,	Wilkinson,
Burke,	Jefferson,	Quitman,	Telfair,	Worth.
Colquitt,	Johnson,			

MARL—is found in—

Bibb,	Clay,	Emanuel,	Pulaski,	Sumter,
Bulloch,	Crawford,	Houston,	Quitman,	Thomas,
Burke,	Dodge,	Jefferson,	Richmond,	Twiggs,
Charlton,	Dougherty,	Laurens,	Schley,	Washington,
Chatham,	Early,	Marion,	Screven,	Wilkinson.
Chattahoochee,	Effingham,	Muscogee,	Stewart,	

GREEN SAND—is found in—

Houston,	Stewart,	Wilkinson,	Twiggs.

MARBLE—is found in—

Catoosa,	Fannin,	Gilmer,	Haralson,	Walker,
Chattooga,	Floyd,	(white and va-riegated.)	Pickens,	(black marble.) Whitefield.

COAL—is found in—

Chattoga,	Dade,	Walker.

BARYTA—is found in—

Bartow,	Murray.

SERPENTINE—is found in—

Fulton,	Rabun,	Taylor,	Troup,	Union.
Gwinnett,	Talbot,	Towns,		

SOAPSTONE—is found in—

Baldwin,	DeKalb,	Fulton,	Heard,	Towns,
Bartow,	Douglas,	Gilmer,	Morgan,	Troup,
Clayton,	Elbert,	Gwinnett,	Murray,	Union,
Cobb,	Fannin,	Habersham,	Paulding,	White.
Coweta	Fayette,	Hall,		

GRANITE—is found in—

Baldwin,	Crawford,	Gwinnett,	Jones,	Rockdale,
Butts,	Dawson,	Habersham,	Madison,	Spalding,
Campbell,	DeKalb,	Hall,	Meriwether,	Talbot,
Carroll,	Douglas,	Hancock,	Monroe,	Taliaferro,
Clarke,	Elbert,	Harris,	Muscogee,	Troup,
Clayton,	Fayette,	Hart,	Oglethorpe,	Upson,

Cobb,	Fulton,	Heard,	Pike,	Walton,
Columbia,	Glascock,	Henry,	Putnam,	Warren,
Coweta,	Greene,	Jasper,	Richmond,	Wilkes.

Granite is found in a number of counties not named in this list. In the above named it can be quarried and used for building purposes,

SANDSTONE—is found in—

Bartow,	Chattooga,	Floyd,	Houston,	Walker.
Catoosa,	Dade,	Gordon,	Jefferson,	

FLEXIBLE SANDSTONE—usually regarded as the matrix of the diamond—is found in Hall, Harris, Heard, Meriwether.

LITHOGRAPHIC STONE is found in Walker.

POLISHING SANDSTONE is found in Bartow, Murray, Whitfield.

FERRUGINOUS SANDSTONE is found in Berrien, Washington.

SILICIFIED CORAL is found in Berrien, Lowndes, Screven, Thomas.

STAUROLITE is found in Fannin—also in a few other counties.

CHLORITE is found in Troup.

KYANITE is found in Carroll, Cherokee, Habersham, Lincoln.

NOVACULITE. is found in Lincoln, McDuffie, Oglethorpe.

PYROPHYLLITE is found in Lincoln.

PYRITE is found in Carroll, Cherokee, Fulton, Haralson, Paulding, Lumpkin, Towns.

AR·ENICAL PYRITES is found in Floyd, Gwinnett, Heard.

LAZULITE is found in Lincoln.

MUCK, for agricultural purposes, is found in Charlton, Clinch, Ware.

TETRADYMITE is found in Lumpkin, Paulding.

WAVELLITE is found in Polk.

The counties of Bryan, Camden, Coffee, Echols, Glynn, Liberty, Montgomery, Pierce and Wayne have not yet been examined by the State Geologist.

FISH AND GAME.

Georgia, extending, as it does, from the Atlantic Ocean to Tennessee, having more than 100 miles of ocean coast, and a multitude of rivers, some flowing into the Atlantic and others into the Gulf of Mexico, affords ample field for fish in great variety. Salt water fish are supplied throughout the year to the interior towns, at reasonable prices. Oysters and other edible shell fish are also supplied in abundance from the coast during the proper season.

The interior streams furnish migratory fish in spring, and fresh water varieties in limited quantity throughout the year. But little has yet been done towards restocking the rivers of the State with food fish, but the public mind is being directed to this point, and the necessary laws will probably soon be enacted.

Game in great variety is found in those portions of the State in which a large part of the forest remains. The principal are quail, duck, wood-cock, pheasant, wild turkey, squirrel, hare, opossum and deer.

There are no general laws of force in the State for the protection of game, and though some have been enacted for the protection of fish, they are practically inoperative.

INDEX.

A

B

F.

G

H

I

J

K

L

M

N

T

U

V

W

Y

Z

ERRATA.

On page 7, the 2nd paragraph, commencing with words, "In nothing regarding us," etc., is the beginni a chapter on CLIMATE. This title was omitted b printer, and not observed by the proof reader, till it wa late to correct it.

On page 36, at the end of the 4th paragraph, the nu of students in the Atlanta University is left *blank*. should have been filled with 244—the number atte the late session.

On the same page, at the end of the 4th line, unde title "Female Colleges," the words "in Georgia" s be *in the world*.

To the list of newspapers in Georgia, (see page and 54) should be added—

Hinesville, (Liberty county)—*Gazette*, weekly.

Dupont, (Clinch county)—*Okeefinokian*, weekly.

Cumming, (Forsyth county)—*Baptist Banner*, wee

MACON—Very earnest, repeated and persistent were made, but without success, to obtain recent re statistics of the city of Macon, before putting this M to press; in consequence of which there are some er the same as they appear on page 91. The population city by recent census is, 9,535 white, and 8,730 black. number of grocery stores given as 6 is a typographical It was intended to be 60. This is probably belo actual number.

The law quoted on page 48 from our latest revised giving the conditions on which aliens and unnaturaliz sons may hold real estate, was repealed by a recent the Legislature. The following is the present law of gia on this subject:

"Aliens, the subjects of Governments at peace w "United States and this State, so long as their Gover "remain at peace, shall be entitled to all the rights "zens of other States resident in this State, and shal "the privilege of purchasing, holding, and conveyir "estate in this State."

This gives to aliens or unnaturalized subjects of Governments, whether resident or not, so long as thei ernments continue at peace with the United States a State, all rights enjoyed by citizens of this State, exe right to vote and hold office, and to perform such civ tions as are confined by law to citizens of this State.

There are some typographical errors, but being o importance, they are not specially noticed.

ERRATA.

On page 7, the 2nd paragraph, commencing with the words, "In nothing regarding us." etc., is the beginning o a chapter on CLIMATE. This title was omitted by the printer, and not observed by the proof reader, till it was too late to correct it.

On page 36, at the end of the 4th paragraph, the numbe of students in the Atlanta University is left *blank*. Thi should have been filled with 244—the number attendin the late session.

On the same page, at the end of the 4th line, under th title "Female Colleges," the words "in Georgia" shoul be *in the world*.

To the list of newspapers in Georgia, (see page 52, 5 and 54) should be added—

Hinesville, (Liberty county)—*Gazette*, weekly.

Dupont, (Clinch county)—*Okeefinokian*, weekly.

Cumming, (Forsyth county)—*Baptist Banner*, weekly.

MACON—Very earnest, repeated and persistent effort were made, but without success, to obtain recent reliabl statistics of the city of Macon, before putting this Manu to press; in consequence of which there are some errors i the same as they appear on page 91. The population of th city by recent census is, 9,535 white, and 8,730 black. Th number of grocery stores given as 6 is a typographical erro It was intended to be 60. This is probably below th actual number.

The law quoted on page 48 from our latest revised Cod giving the conditions on which aliens and unnaturalized pe sons may hold real estate, was repealed by a recent act the Legislature. The following is the present law of Geo gia on this subject :

"Aliens, the subjects of Governments at peace with th "United States and this State, so long as their Governmen "remain at peace, shall be entitled to all the rights of cit "zens of other States resident in this State, and shall hav "the privilege of purchasing, holding, and conveying re "estate in this State."

This gives to aliens or unnaturalized subjects of foreig Governments, whether resident or not, so long as their Go ernments continue at peace with the United States and th State, all rights enjoyed by citizens of this State, except th right to vote and hold office, and to perform such civil fun tions as are confined by law to citizens of this State.

There are some typographical errors, but being of min importance, they are not specially noticed.

www.ingramcontent.com/pod-product-compliance
Lightning Source LLC
Chambersburg PA
CBHW032016010726
47493CB00007B/2422